Therefore

For J... (signed inscription)

Katherine Isaac (signed)

KATHERINE ISAAC

Therefore

It was supposed to be a simple job. Get in. Grab the goods. Get out.
Easy, right?
Not if you're caught by an alpha.

Trystan is all sharp smiles and sharper instincts—an omega thief who's never once been caught. Until now.

Emerson is everything Trystan hates in an alpha: big, bossy, and built like a problem. Unfortunately, he's also the one standing between Trystan and freedom.

A game of cat and mouse turns into something much more dangerous when the heat between them ignites—and neither of them are willing to back down.

He was supposed to steal from the enemy. Not fall into bed with his scent match.

As the job's deadline fast approaches and loyalties are tested, Trystan's worst job may turn out to be the most important of his life.

CONTENT WARNING

Dear Reader,

While I wouldn't class this book as a dark romance, there are a few references and situations that some people may find triggering. If this concerns you, please check the list below before you start reading.

Take care of yourself. No book is worth your mental health.

Love,

Kat xx

Warnings:

- Mentions of childhood abuse

- Mentions of drug abuse

- Kidnapping

- Threats of trafficking and rape

- Gun violence and stabbing

Author's Note

Please note that I am British, and this story is set in the UK, written in British English. There are slight variations in the language between the US and British English.

So manoeuvre your arse and memorise your favourite colour at the theatre.

Aluminium.

Therefore

For the people who answer the question, "What motivates you?"
with one simple word:

Spite.

Chapter One

Trystan

No one noticed me standing against the wall, exactly how I liked it. People scrambled in the street, dashing from place to place, too caught up in their own busy lives to lay their eyes on an unassuming stranger.

It helped, of course, that I had no scent. Omegas were like catnip to an alpha, and I had no intention of being wrapped up in the suffocating arms of an entitled oaf who saw me and my kind as nothing more than a genetically inclined hole to fuck. At least I was taller than the stereotypical omega. Combined with the lack of scent, I easily passed as a beta.

The drawback to my scentless lifestyle was that I now had no sense of smell. Something in the cheap knockoff pheromone suppressants I choked down each day muted my ability to scent those around me. No matter how intensely they extruded their pheromones, no one around me had more scent than a beta. Not the most effective survival technique in my line of work.

The *beep-beep* of an electronic lock from the nearby building entrance narrowed my focus on the crowds. Time to go.

Pushing off the wall, I swerved through the crowd with ease, navigating the currents of people until—

"Ow! Oh no!" a young woman in a baby blue jacket exclaimed as her bags fell to the ground, spilling her belongings across the pavement.

"I'm so sorry!" I dropped to my knees, grabbing various plastic bottles for her to shove back into a tote bag. "Here, let me help."

The surrounding crowds didn't seem bothered by our commotion. Like ants around a fallen leaf, the flow of people continued, caging us in a wall of moving bodies as we collected her things. Cleaning supplies littered the street, most of them used, but luckily the clean cloths were mostly wrapped up, safe from the dirt now coating our knees.

The girl huffed a breath, her cheeks tinged pink. "It's okay, really. I should've been paying more attention."

"Don't worry about it, Abby."

She paused to look at me, her brow furrowed. "How do you know my name?"

I held up a plastic card with a magnetic strip on the back, showing a picture of her smiling face with her name and the words 'Squeaky Cleaners' on the front. "Can't have you losing this."

"Oh! Thank you. Yeah, my boss would kill me if I lost this again."

"Sounds like a real hardass. Got everything?"

Her eyes scanned over the ground as she hefted her bags onto her shoulders. "I think so. Sorry, again."

"It's all good, Abby. Take care now."

I watched her rush away for a moment, making sure she was at least around the corner before I slipped into the alley beside the building I'd seen her exiting. Tossing off my backpack, I quickly pulled a familiar blue jacket out and over my t-shirt. Once paired with a matching baseball cap, Squeaky Cleaners' newest employee was here and ready to get to work. And thanks to the new keycard I pulled out of my sleeve, I'd get inside the building no problem.

Sorry for the switch, Abby. I'll try to return it once I'm done, though.

With Abby's keycard clipped to my jacket, photo-side down, I grabbed my backpack and a bag of cleaning supplies I'd stashed earlier and headed across town to my real target. If I'd timed it right, the building's concierge should be grabbing his lunch when I arrived. One less person to see my face.

My target's neighbourhood was quieter than the city centre I'd started this job in. Sleek buildings brushed the skyline, surrounded by carefully trimmed green spaces that appeared frequently enough to break up the urban jungle. However, it was clear these spaces had only been designed for aesthetics. There weren't any kids playing or couples taking a moment to simply be with each other. No, they were strategically placed to make surrounding businesses look like they cared for more than the money lining their pockets.

After all, how could you be living in a corporate hellscape when you can see a tree from the eighteenth floor?

Pulling out my phone, I double-checked the details from the client. Looked like this was the place. Tapping my stolen card against the reader beside the door, I buzzed into the empty foyer. No security in sight. Perfectly timed. My sneakers squeaked against the polished tile floor as I sauntered to the elevator. Confidence was key if anyone saw me, as was angling my head so the cap hid my face from the cameras. I hit the button to summon the elevator with the tip of my thumb, smudging it against the surface so it wouldn't leave a clear print, then stepped on.

Light jingling music filled the small space, and pretty soon I was striding into the small penthouse foyer. Dodging one more camera with a subtle head turn, I beeped the keycard against the lock and bit my cheek to hold back a grin as the tiny light flicked to green. As I went inside and shut the door behind me, the lock clicking securely back into place, I dropped the bag of cleaning supplies to the floor. Wouldn't be needing that part of the disguise anymore. This was almost too easy.

Considering the client told me my target liked to work from home most days, the penthouse seemed barely lived in. The hallway had a few pieces of art decorating the walls, ink landscapes, the frames dustless and polished. In the lounge, the two sofas looked brand new. Each cushion was fluffed to perfection, not a wrinkle in sight. Shelves were stacked with clothbound books, clearly a fan of the classics, and a vinyl record player was tucked in a corner.

This guy hired a cleaning service every week? I wasn't sure he'd ever heard the word 'clutter'. The dirtiest thing around was a large monstera plant on a side table near the window, and even that was dusted.

But I wasn't here to criticise my target's decorating skills. Though he could really use some statement pieces of colour to brighten up the place.

It didn't take long to track down his home office. One good thing about penthouse jobs was the few rooms to hide things in. And this was the most likely place I'd find the book my client was paying me handsomely to collect.

I didn't have a name for the client. Roman, my boss, handled the negotiations to give both of us privacy and protection. What I had was details on my target, Emerson Richter. Local prosecution lawyer and, judging from his penthouse, joyless drone. If I ever got caught on a job, Emerson was the last person I'd like to see in a courtroom. He had a reputation for finding important details in a case that made things much, much worse for the defendant.

The office was filled with wall-to-wall bookcases, stuffed to the brim with binders, reference books, and boxes.

Yikes, this guy must live for nothing but his job.

He'd left his large wooden desk mostly clear. A small photo of two women and a lamp decorated the space. The fountain pen in the centre was the only sign of recent use. Everything else was safely tucked away onto the shelves or in the desk drawers. But I'd find what I need.

Snapping on a pair of latex gloves from my backpack, I started pulling open the desk drawers and feeling around. No false bottoms that I could see, but the bottom drawer required a key to open. Very promising, but better to check the shelves first, rather than waste time picking the lock if I didn't need to.

The shelves appeared to be arranged by date in some sections and alphabetised in others. Clenching my jaw, I scanned over the F's. The client mentioned the Miranda Fisher case, a huge trafficking operation being tried locally. It was safe to assume she was my client, or at least, someone related to her. The last I'd heard was she'd been detained somewhere, but I couldn't be sure. I made it a point not to look too deeply into the cases surrounding my jobs, or I'd never get anything done.

Having no luck in the L's, I grabbed the first box dated for this year and began rifling through the contents. A lot of files, but nothing I was looking for. Next box.

As time ticked on, my frustration grew, and I yanked my lock-picking kit out of my backpack. Sometimes the obvious solution was the best one.

Taking a deep breath to cool my head and slowly releasing it, I carefully inserted the tension wrench and got to work.

Click. Click. Click. Click.

Damn it, this was taking too long. I supposed I could just break the drawer open, but the client did request stealth. If brute force was more their thing, Leo would've had the job over me. What he lacked in brain cells, he made up for in pure muscular power. Fucking alphas.

This book had better be in this drawer. No one had a desk lock like this for nothing.

I nibbled the corner of my lower lip, focusing hard on the lock that continued to defy me until I finally heard the perfect *CLICK*. The drawer rolled open.

Beep.

I froze, carefully listening for whatever that second sound was. As I heard the distinctive sound of the front door opening, then closing again, my stomach sank to my arsehole.

CHAPTER TWO

EMERSON

I HATED WORKING IN the office. As much as I understood the need for collaboration within a legal team, I'd always been more comfortable in my own space. Having people surrounding me was a distraction.

"No, I didn't do anything fun over the weekend."

"Yes, I am still single and perfectly content that way."

"No, I don't need you to find me a cute little omega to settle down with."

"Yes, I would like you to leave my office so I can get some work done."

My partners at the firm understood my way of working and granted me the flexibility to work where needed, knowing I'd achieve the expected results. But it meant I had to go in for larger meetings at least once a week, on top of my regular in-person meetings with clients.

Luckily, today's client meeting had been unexpectedly cancelled, and I could take my remaining calls from my home office.

I nodded a greeting to Wilson, an older gentleman working as my building's concierge, and stepped onto the elevator. Relief flooded my body. The gentle jingling music soothed my nerves and relaxed my shoulders. Pretty soon, I'd be able to focus in peace.

I slipped my penthouse keycard from my wallet and tapped it against the lock.

Beep.

Home at last.

Wait. Why was there a bag next to the door? Were those cleaning supplies? They looked brand new, still sealed.

Suddenly, my senses were on high alert. Abby usually worked later in the week, so who the hell was wandering around my penthouse?

I quietly placed my satchel on the ground, listening for any movements. Nothing else seemed out of place in the foyer, but as I moved down to my office, I could hear a faint rustling noise and a zipper.

Got you.

The door swung open as I burst into the room, hoping to take the intruder by surprise, only to find a young man with a backpack and blue jacket I recognised, casually admiring my reference books. He turned to me, casually acknowledging my entrance, as though it were totally normal for him to be there.

"Afternoon, Mr Richter! Sorry for the surprise visit." He flashed a charming smile that I saw all the time in courtrooms. It was a smile that said he was harmless. It was all an innocent misunderstanding.

So many of those turned out to be liars.

I eyed him up and down cautiously, taking in the detail of his Squeaky Cleaners jacket—brand new, from the look of it. It was crisp, with folds from the shrink-wrap packaging. Same for the hat.

"I usually don't expect Abby until Thursday."

"She had a family emergency to take care of. It's expected to take the rest of the week," he explained smoothly, but didn't meet my eyes. "This was the only day I could do your weekly service, so here I am."

"Here you are, indeed. But you left your products in the hallway."

His charming smile faltered for the briefest moment. "I only just arrived. Usually with any new client, I like to take a look around first. Makes it easier to prioritise any problem areas, but I got distracted by the impressive collection of books."

I cast my gaze over my office. Nothing seemed out of place until I saw that a box on the shelf had the lid on slightly crooked. Hmm.

The cleaner wasn't exuding any pheromones to indicate fear, but he shuffled his weight between his feet awkwardly. Nervous?

"What did you say your name was?" I asked, flipping the keycard clipped to his jacket to see Abby's smiling face instead of his. "Interesting that you're wearing Abby's keycard."

He stepped away, casually straightening his jacket as he moved towards the door. "Well, I wouldn't be able to get in without it."

"That's true," I conceded, following him closely. "But I'm still waiting for *your* name."

"Do you always walk this close to your cleaners, sir?" he asked, turning to look up at me. His arm brushed against my suit jacket as he turned, leaving a strange tingling heat in its path. "Or am I just special?"

Enough of this.

Taking two large steps, I backed him up against the wall and slammed my hand beside his head, effectively blocking his exit.

His bright green eyes finally met mine arrogantly, almost daring me to do more. He didn't smell like an omega—or anything, actually—but I could admit he was pretty. Wide eyes and pouty lips practically begging to be tasted... or stretched around a cock. I wanted to wipe that smirk off his face, and he'd look so good on his knees.

"Your name. And while you're at it, empty your bag," I growled. This man was an intruder in my home, and I was through with asking.

Instead of answering, the cocky bastard leaned towards me, pressing the length of his body against mine when I didn't move back. Heat flared between us, but I forced myself to ignore it. I wasn't expecting a rut for some time, but that didn't matter now. Unfortunately, he quickly took advantage of the distraction and threw his fist straight into my gut.

As I doubled over, wheezing in a shaking breath, he dashed through the door. Stretching out with one hand, I snatched the backpack and yanked it off his shoulders, but he refused to let it go. Before he could pull away again, I grabbed him in a bear hug and dragged him against me in a tight grip. He twisted in my hold, desperately thrashing his whole body in an attempt to get away and nearly smashing my face with the back of his head.

I snarled in his ear, "What did you take?"

"Fuck you!"

Holding him tighter, I lifted him off the ground so he couldn't get any leverage over me. He was only slightly shorter than me, but he was wriggling hard enough that I was afraid to let up. I just needed to wait him out.

Eventually, his movements slowed, and I held fast, thinking he could be faking in a last-ditch attempt to run. As he fell limp in my arms, I checked his pulse with one hand. Did he pass out?

Fuck. I hadn't lost control of my strength in a long time. What the hell was I supposed to do with him now?

CHAPTER THREE

TRYSTAN

IT WAS SURPRISINGLY NORMAL for me to wake up with my wrists cuffed behind my back. I'd also awoken in my fair share of bathtubs over the years.

Doing both at the same time was a new experience.

Well, this can't be good.

Cracking one eye open, I glanced around the room enough to figure out I was alone. At least I had that going for me. I'd lost the cleaner's jacket and hat at some point in my unconsciousness, and the tub was cool where it touched my cheek. Still, my head felt fuzzy, like it was stuffed with cotton wool. As I tried to stretch out my legs, I realised my ankles were cuffed together and my shoes were gone. Fucking wonderful. No wonder Emerson felt it was safe to leave me alone in here.

Emerson. Shit. How the hell did I mess up badly enough to wind up doing my best impression of a worm in a target's bathroom? He was supposed to be in the office for at least another two hours. Did I miss something when I was preparing?

Maybe Roman should've given the job to someone else. Leo was practically foaming at the mouth to get this job over me, but *no*, I had to fight for this. Should've let Leo end up cuffed in a tub.

He wouldn't have gone as far as tipping Emerson off to spite me, would he? The job would still need to be done, and Emerson would be on alert now. It wouldn't make sense to sell me out.

Screw it. No use worrying about it for now.

My chest ached as I wiggled up to a sitting position and took stock of the situation. Lucky for me, the bathtub was roomy as fuck. I knew Emerson was rich, but even his captive's bathroom was fancy. The light reflecting off the toilet seat looked brighter than my future.

The door had a simple latch on the inside, left unlocked. I supposed I could try to lock it so Emerson couldn't get back in, but it wouldn't do me much good. The only other exit was a small window next to the sink. I was confident in my climbing abilities, but even if I got these cuffs off, escaping to the outside of the eighteenth floor was probably only slightly stupider than shouting for Emerson to run me a bubble bath while I was in here.

There wasn't much else in the room. It was minimalist, much like the rest of the penthouse. Nothing I could use to get out of these cuffs, anyway. If I could find my backpack, I'd have my tools, but Emerson must have stashed it away by now.

As I tested how much I could move in the cuffs, they felt weirdly soft. I guessed they were made of leather, thick and annoyingly secure. I wouldn't be getting out of them with nail clippers. Ignoring the aches in my muscles—How long had I been lying here, anyway?—I pulled my feet under my bum and pushed myself to my feet enough to sit on the rim of the tub.

Okay. Making progress. Now I just had to lift my legs over the edge and swivel—

I landed face down on the bathmat with an undignified crash. Ugh. If Emerson hadn't been on his way to check on me before, he sure was now. Maybe he was wealthy enough to soundproof his captive's bathroom. Did rich people soundproof bathrooms? He had one especially for prisoners, so maybe there was hope.

Rolling onto my back, I waited for a few moments, listening for any movement outside. If Emerson was about to storm in, I had a better chance of fending him off with a well-aimed kick, even with my feet bound. Better than struggling to my feet only to flop on him. Satisfied at the quiet, I moved onto my side and inhaled a deep breath, mentally preparing to get to my feet. The bathroom stank of alpha, and I needed to get out.

Wait. It stank. I could smell that an alpha had been here recently.

Those cheap-as shit-suppressants were wearing off early! Fuck, fuck, fuck! I'd been on those pills for almost a year. There was no telling what could happen if I didn't get another pill down my throat before my pheromones kicked in again. I had to get out *now*.

As I pushed up onto my knees, then my feet—mentally promising myself I'd start stretching before a job from now on—I penguin-shuffled to the door. At least no one was around to see me like this, or I'd never hear the end of it. And if Leo really did sell me out, I was going to kick him in his smug, backstabbing face.

The door squeaked open before I could get to it, and I stepped back, immediately tripping on the ankle-cuffs and falling backwards, "Ah!"

A hand fisting my t-shirt stopped me from hitting the ground again.

"Good to see you're awake."

Emerson's rumbling voice immediately gave me goosebumps. He glared down at me, his icy blue eyes sharp and calculating. Was he debating dropping me the final few feet? Part of me wanted him to get it over with. Helplessly dangling from his grip made me want to scream, but I bit it back.

His arm flexed as he raised me slightly before pausing. "Tell me your name."

I clenched my jaw, staying silent. His scent was overwhelming in person, a tantalising mix of ink and leather underlying his expensive cologne that made me shiver. It was an alpha musk that had my inner omega wanting to curl around him and breathe him in until it consumed my senses. I was in so much trouble.

Emerson flattened his lips into a line and took a breath before trying again. "I asked you a question."

Snapping back to reality, I chuckled, cocking my head to meet his piercing gaze. "And I didn't answer."

His grip tightened on my shirt, whiting his knuckles. I enjoyed knowing I was getting to him so quickly. He seemed like the type who was used to getting what he wanted. If I got him mad, he'd probably trap me back in the bathroom or call the cops. Not ideal situations, but at least I'd get a reprieve from his addicting scent.

"You were much more polite in your little disguise."

"Give me back my jacket, shoes, and backpack, and I'll gladly call you 'sir' again."

He raised an eyebrow. "But would you give me your name? Better yet, tell me who you're working for."

I'd give him my home address, mother's maiden name, and first pet if I breathed him in much longer. Scenting an alpha this closely after months without the sense was messing up my brain. But I could do this. Just hold my stupid omega senses together long enough to get him to leave me alone; then I could figure out an escape plan.

"You may as well drop me back in the tub. I'm not telling you shit."

He studied me for a moment, his pale blue eyes drilling into me as if he could read my desperate thoughts like a book. His arm wasn't even shaking after holding me up this long. How strong was this guy? Strong enough to squeeze me unconscious. Probably strong enough to pin me against a wall while he—

No! None of those thoughts!

A bead of sweat trickled down my spine as heat rose up my neck. My skin itched against my clothes. If I could move my arms, I'd tear my shirt off just to get some air on my skin. Why the hell was Emerson just *staring* at me?

Before I could ask, he hauled me up and over his shoulder, then carried me out of the room with a hand over my thighs.

"What the *fuck*?" I yelled.

"Thought you'd be happy not to be dropped back in the tub, thief."

I lost track of where he was taking me upside down. All I could focus on was the bump of his shoulder against my gut and his mind-blowing scent until he dropped me on something large and soft. A bed? *His* bed?

"Since you insist on not telling me anything useful," Emerson dragged me up the sheets, sitting me at the headboard as he fastened my wrist cuffs to it behind my back. "You can wait here until I'm done with work."

I strained against the cuffs, desperate to find some wiggle room, but they held firmly.

His hand gripped my chin, his skin cool against mine as he forced me to face him. The world seemed to blur around his intimidating frame, and I couldn't look away from his eyes, more pupil than iris. "Now, be honest with me. Are you going to be quiet for a few hours?"

"Are you asking if I'm a screamer, *sir*?" I laughed, practically high on the cocktail of adrenaline and his pheromones.

Emerson released me with a scowl, and I twisted against the bonds again until I ended up lying on my side. The awkward angle pressed my face into the bed, smothered in his scent. The pillows, the sheets, they were all covered in him, and I was practically salivating. My eyes couldn't focus on anything as his musk surrounded me. Everywhere I tried to focus, dizziness and need overtook my mind again. I couldn't breathe properly. The room was too hot for the air to refresh me.

As a hand grabbed my hair and forced my head back, something was shoved into my mouth behind my teeth. Leather dug into my cheeks and realisation surged through the fog in my mind.

A fucking ball gag?!

"Hm. Suits you," Emerson noted as he fastened it behind my head. "I'll be back soon, so you should think about opening up to me. Tell me what I want to know, and I'm sure we can come to an understanding."

Fuck you! I yelled through the gag. I couldn't form the words, but I'm sure he understood the sentiment.

"Let me be clear, *omega*." He leaned down and gripped my jaw again, our faces mere inches apart. "You'll tell me what I want to know. And judging by the state of you, you'll enjoy telling me."

He left the room with the slam of the door, and a lock clicked into place. My heart jack-hammered against my ribs.

He knows I'm an omega.

With him out of the room, my lungs could finally take in air, but I still couldn't cool down. The heat in the room was overwhelming and inescapable. It was coming from me. The bed surrounded me in Emerson's delicious scent, and no matter how much I wriggled and twisted, the damn cuffs didn't have any give. All I could do was writhe on the sheets and scream into the gag as my first heat in almost a year slammed into me like a speeding truck.

How the hell could I escape like this?

CHAPTER FOUR

A

EMERSON

"THANKS, NORAH." I SMILED towards the laptop camera as I scribbled some notes. "Unfortunately, I won't have time to look over Fisher's diary again tonight, but I can review it tomorrow. I'll put in some time for us to catch up again before Detective Rhodes gives us the latest the following day."

Every time I thought I had a handle on this case, something new popped up to make me question everything. But after months of investigating and appeals, the trial date was fast approaching, and we were so close to gathering all the evidence we needed to throw Miranda Fisher behind bars. I couldn't stop now.

Norah leaned into the screen, a mischievous twinkle in her eye. "Oh? Got plans tonight?"

Sure, if questioning the thief who broke into my home office counts as "plans".

Rolling my eyes, I waved away the question. "Shocking, I know."

"I'll say. First time you don't work late in weeks, and it's on some random Tuesday? What are you up to?"

Getting a delicious-smelling omega to give me his name, along with anything else I can get out of him.

"Nothing crazy. I'll speak to you tomorrow."

With the call ended, I leaned back in my office chair, lightly tapping my fingertips on the armrest. It had taken all of my restraint to leave my thief alone while I worked, but my plan required time.

As soon as his pheromone suppressants had started wearing off in the bathroom, I'd scented him as an omega. Not only that, I'd scented him as *mine*.

Finding a scent match—the perfect omega for my inner alpha—was rare and not something I'd ever expected for myself. Even less so during a break-in at my home. The urge to claim him still pulsed through me, but I fought the desire. When I claimed my omega, it would be by his request. Leaving him surrounded by my scent should help him recognise the match and submit to what I can offer him as his alpha.

But then there was the matter of the attempted theft. Besides the fact that no omega of mine would get away with this without a punishment, I still wondered the reason for the break-in.

Reaching into my desk drawer—I'd have to speak to him about picking the lock, as well—I pulled out my thief's backpack and the book he would've got away with had I not been home early. Miranda Fisher's diary was unassuming at first glance, with a plain, hardback green cover and worn corners. The police had granted permission for me to investigate the contents further here, but I hadn't discovered anything new yet.

Flicking through the book lazily, I let my mind wander. Recognisable names, meeting places, and times popped out at me, detailed in scribbled handwriting I'd become all too familiar with recently. Small Post-It notes stuck out from the pages, either highlighting similar entries or linking the same person multiple times.

Why would my omega try to steal this diary? The straightforward assumption would be that he worked with Fisher—likely as someone detailed inside whom the police hadn't put together a full profile for yet. We knew the key players in Fisher's operation, or at least their names, but there was no telling how many strands connected to this web.

Still, why would an omega choose to work with her? It didn't make sense. Unless Fisher, or someone connected to her, hired him to get the diary back. But to what end? The police already had a case built against Fisher and her primary associates. This diary solidified that case, but it didn't introduce anything new. Certainly nothing worth the level of effort my thief went through today.

I'm still missing something.

My vision unfocused as a dull ache thrummed through my head. I massaged my temple with a sigh. Maybe Norah was right. I worked too hard, and really, what did I really have to show for it? The world was better with those criminals behind bars, of course, but maybe it was time to direct my attention towards myself for a change.

My mothers were mated and already had my sister and me by the time they were thirty, with my brother on the way. It was difficult not to be envious of them, as I sat firmly in my late thirties.

Was meeting my omega a sign for me to put aside work and easy beta hookups to finally settle down? I'd have to convince him first. Something told me my fated omega wouldn't feel inclined to listen, but I'd never met a challenge I couldn't dominate.

Warmth flooded my chest, down to my throbbing cock. Ever since I'd recognised that omega's delectable mint and metallic scent, my body refused to relax. My inner alpha knew what I needed, and he was tied up in my bedroom, surrounded by my scent.

Mine. Protect. Fuck. Bite. Claim.

The thoughts raced around my mind until attempting to work became pointless. I'd waited for long enough.

My heart pounded a rapid beat as I fired off a text to my assistant and sealed the diary in a large envelope, leaving it on my desk. Once I'd grabbed a bottle of water from the fridge, I marched down the hallway to my bedroom. With each stride, a fresh, earthy scent filled my nostrils. Minty, with a sharp metallic undertone and something smoky and alluring. Vetiver. I never wanted to inhale anything else.

As I twisted the key in the lock and tore open the door, the mouthwatering scent sucker-punched my senses. The overwhelming intensity of it almost brought me to my knees as I locked eyes with the source of the scent. My omega. He lay where I left him, more or less. The sheets were scrunched around his body, and the pillows had been knocked to the floor. Interestingly, he held a bedside lamp in the air between his now sockless heels, the cord taut until he yanked it from the wall.

I waved the bottle of water. "And here I was, coming to reward you for staying put this time."

With a sharp twist of his body, the lamp crashed into the wall beside me. At least his aim was off. Pity about the dent in the wall, though.

"Done?" I asked, raising an eyebrow. "Or are you planning to kick your socks at me next?"

My omega glared daggers at me, his chest heaving and cheeks flushed red. It thrilled me to see he hadn't lost his fire. He was gorgeous, enraged, and vulnerable.

His dilated eyes followed me as I circled the bed to the corner where his head lay. As though I'd crossed an invisible barrier, he shot up to a sitting position, leaning away from my outstretched hand as far as he could.

I held my hands up in surrender. "Relax, omega. I'm just removing the gag. Unless you'd prefer to keep it on?"

He eyed me suspiciously but made no move to avoid me this time.

Good. Maybe he can be reasoned with, after all.

"Lean forward for me," I said, reaching around his head to remove the gag, along with the loop connecting his cuffs to the headboard.

Guilt twinged in my chest as he opened and closed his mouth, stretching his jaw now that he could finally move. The restraints had been necessary, though. There was no chance I'd have made it through my calls with him screaming the building down and destroying more of my furniture in here.

Twisting the seal off the water, I held the bottle to his lips. "Here, drink this."

Green eyes flicked to the hand holding the cap, and he accepted the offering. A trickle of water escaped the corner of his mouth as he drank, and I ached to lick it off his skin. However, I settled for wiping it with my shirt sleeve before rolling them up to my elbows, setting the remainder of the water on the bedside table.

He leaned back against the single remaining pillow by the headboard, practically relaxed compared to how I found him a moment ago. "So, do you gag every guest in your bedroom, or am I just lucky?"

"Calling yourself a 'guest' here implies there was an invitation."

"Hm?" He blinked at me. "Oh, sorry. Zoned out for a second there. I was having a flashback of being forced into this room and tied to the damn bed. You're a lawyer, right? Last I checked, keeping a hostage is pretty fucking illegal."

"So is breaking and entering. The way I see things, I could call my friends in the police department and have them come pick you up. I'm sure a pretty omega with a delectable scent like yours will make plenty of friends behind bars."

His jaw ticked, and the glare was back in full force.

"Or you can answer my questions. In return, I'll let you go and help you ride out your heat."

"You'll 'help me with my heat'? How *generous* of you." He scoffed, eyes refusing to meet my gaze. "Hate to disappoint, but I'm not in heat. My cheapass suppressants wore off, is all."

"Deny it all you like, but your scent doesn't lie. Not to mention..." I placed a hand on his forehead, not deterred by him trying to lean away. His skin was hot and clammy under my palm. "You're burning up. It won't be long before you're delirious."

While triggering his heat had never been my intention when locking him in a room filled with my scent earlier, I couldn't deny that the result pleased me to no end. Watching my feisty omega slowly come undone before my eyes was mesmerising.

My hand moved up from his forehead into his hair, letting the soft locks run through my fingers. Despite his initial recoil at my touch, this time he allowed it. He glared determinedly at the wall opposite him, but as I continued to touch him, his jaw steadily relaxed, and his scowl softened slightly.

Pride surged in my chest. Taking care of my omega, relaxing him, and easing his tensions was what my alpha was born to do. Looking after my omega was the only thing that mattered.

"I understand that you're loyal to whoever sent you here, but like it or not, your heat has started. You can swallow handfuls of suppressants like M&M's, but it's not going to stop now. You won't make it down the block without someone sniffing you out and calling the police. Therefore, it's in your best interest to let me help you."

"Are you kidding?" He whirled around, rising onto his knees to gain some height on me, even in his prone state. "I'm dead if I sell them out! I don't care how good you alphas smell, it's not worth my life. *Therefore* you can suck my dick out of the kindness of your heart before I give you *anything*."

"I'm beginning to regret removing that gag."

Giving him a moment to think he had one over on me was completely worth it, just to see that smirk wiped from his face.

In a smooth movement, I knocked him off balance and had him lying face-down on the sheets, with me straddling the back of his thighs. Turning his head to the side, he squirmed uselessly beneath me as I pinned him in place, leaning down to lightly brush my lips over his neck and inhale his addicting scent where it was strongest. His pulse thumped against my barely there lips, mint radiating from his heated skin, laced with vetiver and something metallic.

His earthy essence allowed my alpha to finally *breathe*. This was where I was meant to be.

"Allow me to make something clear to you, omega." I spoke against his neck, working my way up to his ear. "I am your alpha. Therefore, your safety and wellbeing are now my responsibility. And I will not have you suffer through a heat out of your own stubbornness. Do you truly expect me to believe that if I checked your needy little hole, I wouldn't find it dripping with slick right now?"

He shivered beneath me, wriggling in a futile attempt to get away, but only managing to rub his arse and bound hands against my front. A small moan escaped him, and he muffled it against the sheets.

Fisting a hand in his hair, I pulled his head up enough to turn him to look at me. "No, let me hear you. I don't want to miss a single noise you make."

This time, he didn't look away. His bright green eyes had darkened to a deep emerald, only visible as a sliver of iris around his dilated pupils, glazed over in a primal need.

"Do you feel this?" I ground my crotch into his hands, surprised when he gripped my cock through my trousers.

His fingers explored my length, rubbing the girth under his palm. I'd grown painfully hard breathing him in this close, desperately waiting for him to accept his heat and me.

"It's all for you. You're the only one who gets this knot." I muttered into his ear, biting the lobe to make him squirm against me again. "I know you'll take it so well."

He let out a soft whimper, barely a noise at all. I would have missed it had our faces not been close enough for our breaths to mingle. The desperate sound sparked a lust inside me I'd never felt before. It would be so easy to kiss him. To taste him.

But I needed him to want it.

Reaching my other hand around him, I sat back on my knees and pulled his torso up against me. My heart pounded in my chest so hard I wondered if he could feel it against his back. He settled against me, feeling for the tent in my trousers again. His hands were magic, even when cuffed. I couldn't wait to be inside him.

As I released his hair, letting his head rest against my shoulder, both of my hands roamed his chest under his t-shirt. His breath hitched when I found a pair of nipple piercings and circled them before gently pinching.

"Harder..." He gasped.

I rolled them between my fingers, enjoying how his hips twitched in a silent plea for friction. "Tell me your name, omega."

Hair tickled my face as he shook his head. "You'll have to do better than that, *sir*."

I pinched down hard. "Your mouth is going to get you into trouble."

"Feels like I'm already in trouble." He squeezed my cock through my trousers again.

"Is that what you want?" Tugging his jeans open with one hand, I pulled out his hard cock, already leaking precum. I gave him a light, teasing stroke. "You want to be stretched on your alpha's knot like a good omega?"

He thrust into my hand, whining, "Please..."

"Tell me your *name*."

His chest heaved in my arms, and he turned his head to face me. Forest green eyes studied my face, eventually settling on my lips. As my thumb swiped over the head of his cock, he closed the gap between us and kissed me.

"Trystan." He spoke against my lips. "My name is Trystan."

A grin broke across my face. At last, my omega had a name.

"Trystan," I repeated, planting a soft kiss on his lips, then his temple, and continuing to stroke him, faster now. "Come for me."

He obeyed without hesitation, gasping beautifully and pulsing in my hand like waiting for those words had been the only thing holding him back. His vetiver scent filled the room, the smokiness intensifying like a bonfire as it consumed my senses.

As Trystan relaxed against my chest, his face in the crook of my neck, my alpha growled beneath my skin.

Mine.

CHAPTER FIVE

TRYSTAN

H EAT BURNED AT MY cheeks as I struggled to catch my breath after my release.

I could have given Emerson a fake name, but honestly, the thought hadn't even crossed my mind. The rumble of his voice in my ear sent tingles down my spine with every word, and part of me had ached to hear my name on his lips. Now that I knew what it sounded like, I wanted it again.

My biceps throbbed, the cuffs around my wrists forcing them into an awkward angle that I'd be feeling for days. I needed to get out of these fucking cuffs. Then I could finally touch more than the tent in his trousers. His hair looked so soft. Just long enough to grab onto and pull into another kiss. He'd tasted so good on my lips, a mix of coffee and his own underlying alpha scent. If I turned my head and leaned back, I could reach him again and—

Damn it, I was supposed to be escaping him. Stupid omega brain!

But that didn't make sense. If I ran out of here, I wouldn't get to feel Emerson's hard chest against my back anymore. His comforting lips on my forehead. His large hand around my cock.

A cramp pulsed through my abdomen, my inner omega desperately screaming for more attention from the alpha surrounding me in his scent. That handjob had barely scratched the surface of my need, and Emerson knew it. I was still hard in his hand, loosely held as his other hand teased over my nipple piercing again.

"You did so well, Trystan," he muttered, peppering light kisses over my jaw and neck. "So good for your alpha."

The words warmed my heart, filling my chest with pride. I'd always fought the omega desire to please an alpha, avoiding them even during my heats, but I couldn't deny the pleasure that surged through every fibre of my being.

"Fuck me," I breathed. "Take off the cuffs and give me your knot. I know you want to."

He chuckled in my ear, "Oh, I'd like nothing more than to fill you with my cum and ease your heat. But after the stunts you've pulled today, I think I'll take my time with you."

Before I could bite back, my cum-stained shirt landed on the duvet as Emerson pushed me face down onto the bed, then pulled my hips up and my jeans down. Cool air met my bare arse, leaving me squirming in my vulnerable position.

"Look at you," Emerson said from behind me. "I knew you were needy, but all this slick coming out of you..." A hot tongue slid over my exposed hole, dragging a low moan from my throat. "So beautiful."

He descended on me like a beast tearing into its prey. Hands spread my cheeks apart, squeezing the flesh as his tongue swirled around my rim, eventually dipping inside. My hips bucked against his face, and my mind went blank. The only thing I could focus on was the sensation of his tongue eating me out like I was his last meal.

"Emerson... Fuck me," I breathed out a moan. "I need more."

A sharp smack cracked across my arse.

"You have a lot to learn about respecting authority, don't you?"

"If I say 'yes', will you fuck me already?"

Another slap.

"Ah!" I yelped as his hand massaged over my cheek, soothing the burn. "Will you fuck me already, *sir?*"

"Getting there."

I could practically hear his smug smirk before he spanked me again. The sound echoed around the room before ringing out again and again, each slap dragging more embarrassing gasps and moans from my lips.

Getting away was impossible. Any time I managed to wiggle an inch away, his large hands pulled me back and licked over my hole again. Emerson's torturous tongue lapped at the slick

35

dribbling down to my balls, sucking each one into his mouth before spanking me again.

My cheeks burned, spreading down to my upper thighs. As I wiggled in the restraints, slowly gaining more leverage—probably from sweat—my cock throbbed between my legs, painfully hard and leaking precum.

"Do you want me to *apologise* for breaking in? Is that what this is?" I panted, barely getting a sentence out before huffing in another wanton breath. "Because I won't. It was just a job! I don't meet my clients. I don't even know their names. I only work as a third party. Now *please,* will you *fuck me, Alpha*?"

The spanking stopped, his fingers lightly trailing over my behind. Each touch burned like the lick of a flame, making me twitch against him. His thumb circled my hole, barely applying the pressure my omega craved before slipping inside with ease.

"Good boy, Trystan." Emerson leaned over me and pressed his lips to my temple, his thumb pushing into me further, gently moving around inside. "Now, I'm going to fuck you. I'm going to stretch this little hole until you can take my knot, and you're going to ride out your heat seated on my cock, stuffed full of my cum. Is that what you want?"

I whimpered. Fucking *whimpered.* Emerson had me exactly where he wanted me, and this time, I couldn't wait for him to live up to his promises.

He smoothed a hand under my shirt, down my spine. "Use your words, darling. Or I'll have to sto—"

"I want it!" Twisting my head around, I met his eyes over my shoulder. "Please, Alpha."

This time, Emerson was the one to kiss me. Fully dominating my mouth with soft lips and a wicked tongue that had my toes curling. His cool leather scent deepened as I consumed more of him. Layers of earthy, spicy patchouli and a soft wave of vanilla that warmed my chest. It was like nothing I'd smelled or felt before. A sense of belonging. Not *to* someone exactly, but *with* them.

Was this what people meant when they talked about scent matches?

I wiggled my butt as Emerson removed his thumb from me. When it wasn't immediately replaced with fingers, panic shot through me. "No, no, please! I said I want it."

"Shh, trust me for a moment." He kissed my forehead, then the corner of my eye. I hadn't even realised a tear had formed. "Trust your alpha."

The tension in my arms released, and cool air kissed my wrists, followed by my ankles.

"Be careful. You might be sore for a while," Emerson said, tossing the cuffs onto the floor.

Moving slowly, I rolled onto my back beneath Emerson and stretched my arms up, my back cracking in just the right way. Fuck, that felt good. And now I could finally touch him the way I wanted.

This was my chance to escape.

Emerson was so relaxed. A quick backhand or kick to the head is all it would take. The key was still in the door, so I could lock him in and just keep running. Stairs would probably be faster than the elevator. I'd be out on the street in minutes. Maybe the police would pick me up, but I could figure something out.

Reaching up with one hand, my fingers trailed across Emerson's jaw. His five o'clock shadow tickled my fingertips as I took in his icy blue eyes, which bored deep into my own.

It would be so easy.

Gripping his hair in one hand, I made my choice. With a sharp tug, our mouths met, and I was bathed in his warm vanilla scent again. My spare hand fumbled with his shirt buttons, desperately pulling to expose more of his skin until impatience got the better of me. Buttons flew over the bed. Ignoring Emerson's tutting, my hand explored his exposed chest. His arm snaked under my thigh, pulling my leg out of my jeans where they'd been trapped around my knees.

As his kisses trailed down my throat, his hand returned to my arse and carefully inserted two fingers. An obscene squelch reached my ears, and my breath left my lungs as his fingers curled and twisted inside me.

Precum dripped onto my stomach, my cock screaming for friction. A brush of his fingertips against my prostate had my back arching off the bed, a low moan rippling out of me.

"There! Oh, that's so fucking good!"

"Mm, but still so tight for me." Emerson licked along my collarbone, attacking the spot inside me with vigour. "Need to open you up for my cock. Do you even want my knot, Trystan?"

I nodded frantically. I'd never wanted anything more in my life.

"Give it to me. Stuff me full. I need it. I need you, please. Please make me come," I babbled, my brain focused entirely on the need radiating from my every pore.

"I've got you," he promised, inserting a third finger and aiming straight for my prostate again.

Lips covered my own, and my body convulsed beneath him. Cum spurted between our chests as he ripped my orgasm out of me mercilessly.

"That's it, love," he muttered against my neck. "I want you to come as many times as you need tonight. This is all for you, my omega."

With another kiss to my forehead, gently easing me down from my orgasm, Emerson removed his fingers and sat up on his knees. Reaching into a side drawer, Emerson pulled out a small bottle of lube and tossed it onto the one remaining pillow. Pulling his shirt off his shoulders, he said, "You look so beautiful like this, but I want you naked when I take you."

We removed the last of our clothing, hastily throwing them onto the floor, then collided with each other yet again. The drying cum on our chests didn't matter. It would only get worse.

Emerson's well-muscled body covered mine, pressing me into the mattress. He almost made me feel dainty beneath him, despite us being so close in height. That side of an alpha had never appealed to me before, but right now, my omega was practically purring.

He hoisted my leg over his hip and generously coated his length in the lube before rubbing the head against my entrance. The brief cold made me jump, but feeling how much thicker Emerson's cock was compared to his fingers had me half-hard again.

"Don't keep teasing me, Emerson." I spoke through a half-lidded gaze that I hoped was seductive instead of just desperate and exhausted. "Another heat spike is going to hit me any second, and I wanna be full of cock when it does."

"Good to know some of your plans aren't awful," Emerson teased as he finally entered me.

"Mm, ah! Fuck!" I crossed my ankles behind him, pulling him deeper. "And here I thought that getting caught"—I gasped as he ground his hips against mine, pushing in further—"during my heat, was a great idea."

"I won't lie"—he pushed in another inch, before pulling out, then going in further again—"I'm thoroughly enjoying your terrible plan."

Each thrust of his hips pushed him in more, stretching me wider around his girth. The stretch burned in that perfect way my omega ached for. And my alpha had barely got started.

As I slowly accommodated the girth inside me, Emerson picked up a rhythm that had my inner omega mewling in pleasure.

Fuck, those noises were coming from me.

His arms coiled around me, and my moans were muffled against his neck. That spicy patchouli scent surrounded me, making my mouth water. I licked a long stripe up his neck, the salt of his sweat mixing with his delicious scent, and he moaned low in his throat. Easily the sexiest sound I'd ever heard and one I was determined to hear again.

My hips bucked, meeting his thrusts until his hands lifted both my legs onto his shoulders. He leaned down, practically folding me in half, and licked into my mouth. As his weight shifted, every roll of Emerson's hips had his cock punching my prostate and stars dancing behind my eyelids.

Fisting the sheets above my head, all coherent thoughts escaped me. I muttered attempts at words, but my mind was a mess of sensations. Patchouli and warm vanilla. Smacking skin echoing around the room. The growing fire in my abdomen as the cock impaling me moved faster and faster.

"You're so tight. So fucking perfect," he growled, biting my lower lip before swallowing down my groan. "But I've got more to give you."

His movements stuttered and increasing pressure around my hole told me exactly what was happening. Emerson's knot was inflating, preparing to lock us together for minutes, or maybe hours, as he pumped his seed into me. It was what my omega craved most. What I'd been aching for since my heat began.

"Give it to me," I gasped. "I need it."

Emerson pulled all the way out, panting for a moment, before flipping me onto my hands and knees and landing a smack onto my already stinging arse.

"Haven't you learned yet, omega?" Emerson chuckled, running the length of his cock between my cheeks until I could feel the burning heat of his rapidly inflating knot against my twitching hole. "You know what to say."

"Please, Alpha." I whimpered, looking at him over my shoulder. "Please give me your knot."

His slick chest covered my back, and our lips crashed together. In my next breath, Emerson rammed back inside me to the hilt, straight at my prostate, his knot stretching me more than I'd thought possible. Within a few shallow pumps, I was coming with my cock untouched. My inner muscles squeezed his shaft, dragging Emerson into his own orgasm and milking him of his cum. Our moans mixed together in a cacophony of pleasure until we could only gasp for air, still locked together below the waist.

Emerson dragged me down to lie on my side with him, one arm beneath my head and the other smoothing over my abdomen. I could still feel him inside me, his swollen cock twitching as he continued to release into me.

I didn't know how long the reprieve from my heat would last. What I did know was that my inner omega was only partially sated. Pretty soon, another spike would hit me, and I'd need more.

Part of me couldn't wait.

CHAPTER SIX

EMERSON

I T WASN'T SURPRISING TO see the empty space next to me when I woke up. What did surprise me was finding my wrists cuffed to the headboard.

Oh, he'll pay for that later.

With a pinch and twist of my fingers, I had my wrists free. I still couldn't believe Trystan hadn't figured out there was an emergency release. Although in fairness, the cuffs were a special order, and he'd been pretty distracted by an unexpected heat.

Rolling out of bed, I left the sheets as they were. I wanted Trystan's smoky vetiver scent to linger a little longer before I cleaned up. Maybe I'd keep a pillowcase until he was back in my bed. A smile stretched across my face. I wasn't even mad Trystan was gone. I knew the risk as soon as I uncuffed him. But I had his name and something he wanted. We'd meet again very soon.

As I headed for the kitchen, I scrolled through my phone's notifications. Plenty of emails, as usual. But two texts from my assistant, Pearl, stood out:

Transferred evidence back to the office. Usual place.

Don't ask me to come over like that again. I can never unhear those sounds.

I made a mental note to send her flowers and a spa day voucher soon. This wasn't in her job description, but there was no one I trusted more to deal with the transfer. At least, not without Norah ripping into me at every opportunity.

Speaking of the devil, Norah's name flashed across my screen.

"Good..." I checked the time on the screen. Two-thirty. Crap. "Afternoon. How can I help?"

"Pearl said you were taking a sick day, but I don't buy it," Norah snapped, clearly not in the mood for fun pleasantries. "You're the healthiest person I know. So tell me what's going on."

I grabbed a fresh bottle of water from the fridge and headed back to my bedroom. "I'm allowed to take a sick day, Norah."

"If you were genuinely sick, I'd agree with you. Don't make me ask again."

The joys of dealing with another alpha.

Sighing, I sat on the edge of my bed. "Someone broke in yesterday. I had to deal with it."

Norah's voice immediately softened. "Are you okay? Did they get away with anything?"

"I'm fine. They got away, but I know what they were after—Fisher's diary. What I don't know is who told them I had it."

"Think we have a leak?"

"Us, or the police," I admitted. "I checked the evidence out formally, so there's an easy paper trail if someone knows where to look."

Norah went quiet for a moment, but I could hear her typing on her laptop. "Okay. Is the diary still with you?"

"No. Pearl collected it last night and returned it to the office. It's safe. You can check with her."

"Perfect. Do the police have any leads on our thieves?"

My chest tightened as I pictured Trystan's face beneath me, deep in ecstasy. He was our thief, but not the source of the crime. If I could find out who he worked for, who requested the job, I could bypass an arrest for him altogether. At the very least, negotiate on his behalf.

"I didn't report it."

"You, what?!"

"The police could be the leak, Norah. You said it yourself."

"So you got your damn PA to move it instead?" Norah growled, her alpha rage palpable even over the phone.

I took a breath. My inner alpha never responded well to other alphas asserting dominance, but I respected Norah as my boss and friend. If only my alpha would remember that.

"I had other things to take care of." I spoke slowly, calmly. "And Pearl is as loyal as they come. You know that."

"I *know*." Norah huffed. "This situation just doesn't sit well with me. We're supposed to be wrapping up this case.

Targeting the diary now doesn't make sense, especially not with everything else we have. The evidence against Fisher is irrefutable, and the police already checked over the diary. Anything new we find would just be a bonus."

"We need to talk to detective Rhodes again. He's been on this case from the very beginning. We can trust him."

More clicks on the keyboard. "We have that meeting with him tomorrow. Make sure you're there."

"Of course."

"And, y'know, feel better or whatever." Norah tsk-tsked. I could almost feel her disapproving glare from across the city.

Guilt panged through my chest. I couldn't tell her Trystan was the thief. My nature wouldn't allow me to put him at risk in any way. But there were other ways of letting her in.

"I've met my scent-match," I admitted, smiling to myself at the sound of Norah's gasp through the phone. "He went into heat after the break-in, and I had to take care of him."

"Emerson, that's..." Norah paused, then laughed. "Oh, wow. You really had a hell of a night, didn't you? I want the whole scent-match story, but I'm assuming you should get back to him."

Well, funny story, actually. He cuffed me to my bed and ran out while I was asleep, and I have no idea where he is. It's all going really well.

"Thank you. Sorry for being secretive."

I meant it, too. Norah didn't deserve these secrets, but I had to protect my omega. I told him he was my priority now, and I didn't take that lightly.

"I'd probably do the same in your position. I get territorial any time someone so much as looks at Frankie. If he were an omega on top of that, in *heat*." She let out a low whistle. "Dangerous. Hope I get to meet him soon, though."

"You will. He'll be in my life as long as I'm breathing."

Trystan may not fully understand it yet—if he did, he wouldn't have run off—but now that I knew he existed, he'd never be rid of me. I'd call in every favour, do everything in my power to protect him, whether he liked it or not.

All I had to do first was find him.

CHAPTER SEVEN

TRYSTAN

EXPERIENCING A HEAT WITHOUT an alpha was agony. Hours, sometimes days, of a burning need that was never quite sated. But when I'd woken up with a semi-clear mind for the first time in hours, I forced myself to get out of Emerson's penthouse before another spike hit me. Riding it out in my shitty flat wasn't ideal, but I had a system: give my flatmate my phone and get them to lock me in the bathroom, throw in some energy drinks and snacks, run a cold bath with the most overpowering bath salts hands could steal, and spend some quality time with a knotted dildo.

Classy? Not even a little. But fucking effective.

Now that the worst was over, my body had cooled to a regular temperature, and I could finally appreciate a warm shower. I scrubbed my skin until it was as red as my arse and the water ran cold.

Eventually, I called it quits and dried myself, pulling on a comfy old pair of sweatpants that wouldn't irritate my

49

still-sensitive skin. The shower helped me feel more like myself again, but I could still smell leather and patchouli on my skin. The scent of an alpha. Emerson.

I scrubbed a hand down my face with a groan. He'd been living rent free in my mind ever since I got out of the penthouse. At least I'd had some fantasies to dip into for the rest of my heat. Getting knotted by a dildo was enough to quiet my inner omega for a few minutes. A real alpha's knot turned out to be so much better than I imagined. I almost wanted to kick myself for avoiding it for so long. Emerson was responsible for the best orgasms of my life, and part of me wished I never left.

If he'd had his way, I'd probably still be there. And if I were an honest man, I'd be willing to admit part of me wasn't mad at that idea.

Too bad I steal for a living.

That was something I hadn't considered. Emerson was more than happy to help his omega and make all the sweet promises of priorities and care, but it was literally his job to put me in jail.

Grinding my teeth, I ran a hand through my hair, pulling at the ends. If my life insisted on being a fucking joke, it should at least be funny.

Gulping down the last of a lukewarm energy drink, I went looking for my flatmate, Bee. We'd been friends since our early teens, though Bee had been smart enough to stay away from Roman's shady deals. Instead of engaging in theft the old-fashioned way, like me, they liked to make rent by hacking information, then selling it to the highest bidder. The only reason I didn't wholly approve of their method was because I wasn't patient enough to sit and do that myself. I preferred the adrenaline of the hands-on approach, though I appreciated Bee's assistance from time to time.

I called out, "Hey, Bee! What time is it? How long have I been out?"

Bee looked up from their laptop, their scraggly copper hair sticking up in every direction and the screen's light reflected in their glasses. "Almost midnight, so only about eighteen hours. Surprised to see you up so soon."

"Good to see you, too," I muttered dryly, though I wasn't lying. Bee could see through that shit too easily. "Any news?"

"Like in the world or specifically from Roman? Because, yes." They rolled their chair away from the desk, leaning back in a stretch that had their back cracking like a glowstick. "You had a text a few hours ago. Said to hurry it up or... Well, I'm not comfortable repeating the threat. Go ahead and use your imagination, then make it a lot worse."

Picking up my phone from the desk, I flopped across our questionably stained sofa and read Roman's message. Fuck. He wasn't kidding around this time. Looked like the client was pressuring him on top of the usual turnaround time. Who the hell was so desperate for that book? The job outline said it had already been in police custody for weeks.

I stared at the ceiling, tapping my phone against my chin as I relayed the message to Bee. "Doesn't look like he knows exactly what happened yesterday—"

"You mean you going into heat and begging the target to fucking rail you?"

One of these days, I'll learn to keep my mouth shut around Bee.

"—but he's sent an updated location of the book," I finished. "Also, Leo's apparently getting ready to step in if I don't get it done, as per fucking usual."

Bee stood, joining me on the sofa by lifting my legs and sitting with them on their lap. They tapped a rhythm on my shins, deep in thought. "Is Leo the huge one who broke your nose last year?"

"That's him."

"The one who's further up Roman's butt than that alpha was up yours this time yesterday?"

A swift heel jabbed into Bee's gut was my response. Little jerk got away with way too much.

Chuckling to themself, Bee turned their head to me and asked, "In all seriousness, do you have a plan for how to get that book? He's gonna be expecting you this time."

I nodded. "That's why I have to strike his office tomorrow morning. He won't expect me there so soon. I'll probably need your help this time, if you're up for it."

"An in-person job?" Bee grinned at me. "For you? I suppose I could be persuaded."

Matching their grin, I sat up and clasped their shoulder. "You do make a wonderful distraction."

We had a plan. Or at least, the bones of a plan.

I'd never fucked up a job this badly, let alone literally. But now that I was back in my element, with Bee at my side, the strategy flowed, and things started coming together. By the time we were ready, we had a few hours to rest up, then it was off to work.

Emerson wouldn't know what hit him.

CHAPTER EIGHT

EMERSON

I F ONE MORE PERSON interrupted me today, I was going to lose it. This was exactly why I preferred working from home—no distractions, unless a thieving omega was nearby. But today, everyone and their great-aunt seemed to need my attention.

"I'm not looking over the case file, Harris. That trial isn't for another two weeks," I growled at my friend, my poker face long abandoned.

Unfortunately, Harris had seen worse from me over years of working together and wasn't easily deterred. "Come on, please. I need your eyes on this, or the guy's gonna walk. We all know he did it but—"

"But right now, it isn't the priority," I snapped. "I'll get to it, really, just not today."

Harris sighed, folding his arms over his chest and staring me down. For a beta, he had incredible confidence standing up to alphas. Usually, that confidence worked for our friendship, keeping me on my toes, but today was not the day for it.

After a long moment, he finally relented. "Okay, go do your thing. I'll grab you after, and you can fill me in on the latest with the Fisher case." He turned to leave before adding, "Oh, and thanks for stealing my favourite board room for that client meeting in an hour, by the way. You know I like to spread out in there for cases like this one. It's way roomier than my cupboard-sized office."

"The what—" I started, but he'd already escaped my office. Poking my head out of the doorway, I asked Pearl, "Why does Harris think I have a client meeting today?"

She blinked up at me, her blond eyebrows raised. "Because you do. I'd assumed you were the one who added it to your calendar this morning. It's short notice, but not unheard of."

I shook my head, grinding my teeth before catching myself and taking a deep breath. My calendar was supposed to be blocked out until the meeting with Norah and detective Rhodes this afternoon. Something was up. The timing felt too strange to be a coincidence.

Pearl clicked on her laptop a few times. "The notes say it's for a new case being brought in, but there's not much other information." She narrowed her eyes, thinking for a moment before snapping out of her little trance. "Oh, that reminds me. I have that *file* you requested."

Pearl met my gaze, her large innocent eyes twinkling with barely contained mischief. She was always happy to help with research, but she especially loved anything off the books. Said it made her feel like a secret agent in an old noir movie.

Smiling, I nodded to my office and headed back inside. Once Pearl joined me, locking the door behind her, and I sat behind my desk then said, "Please tell me you found something."

Pearl smiled widely, handing me a thick manila folder. "It took a lot of digging, but I present to you: Trystan Wells. Age twenty-five."

Twenty-five?! Ugh, I'm practically a cradle-robber.

She continued, "I have to say, this omega of yours is excellent at covering his tracks, but no one's perfect."

"Except you." I chuckled, flicking the folder open.

My eyes immediately caught on a blurry CCTV image of a young man glaring up towards the camera. It was dated several years ago. He couldn't have been older than fifteen. His black hair was longer, with a jagged fringe covering one eye, but even blurred I recognised the scowl painted across his face.

"He seemed to be quite the little rebel in his teen years. Started with vandalism, then moved on to shoplifting and a few car jacks for added spice," Pearl commented. "But strangely, his record quickly cleans up remarkably well. Looks like he really turned his life around—on paper, at least."

"Or he was just more experienced and learned to hide better."

"More than likely, considering your run-in with him."

I studied the pictures first, none of them recent. The latest was three years old, taken at a hospital where he sat in a waiting room, cradling his right arm. My blood boiled seeing him in obvious pain, even in an old photograph.

"His hospital records tell more of a story than his criminal record. For what it's worth, I don't recommend reading them, even though I know you will." Pearl's heels clicked towards the door until she closed it behind her, leaving me alone with the folder.

She was right on all counts. It was filled with seemingly endless entries of broken bones, fractures, deep lacerations requiring stitches all throughout his childhood, from toddler years to early-teens. If I'd read these records on behalf of a client, I'd feel sick. Reading them and knowing the man involved, caring for him, made me want to burn the fucking world.

Eventually, I leaned back in my chair, pinching the bridge of my nose and inhaling a long, deep breath. There was nothing I could do about the past. I thought I'd come to terms with that in my line of work, but it felt so much more personal with Trystan. With my omega. A few quick searches confirmed his mother died almost ten years ago and his father went shortly after. Drug abuse. At least they were dead and gone. If I'd been able to meet them...

My inner alpha bristled against my mind, aching to protect him. I'd settle for making sure nothing like that ever happened to him again. He may not have taken my role as his alpha seriously when we spoke, but I meant every word I said to him.

Turning to the final page in the folder, my interest piqued. Another CCTV photo, this time outside the hospital, dated four years ago. Trystan was standing in the car park, speaking to a bald man leaning out of the driver's side window of a classic Ferrari. His stance was awkward, leaning away from the car. I'd bet money Trystan wasn't enjoying this conversation. Focusing on the stranger, the camera angle didn't allow me to see his face and his head tattoo was blurred to hell.

But the car's licence plate was perfectly legible.

Scribbling the details on a Post-It, I checked the time and groaned. Time for my mysterious client meeting. At least I'd still have time afterwards to review the diary before seeing Norah and Rhodes.

As I exited my office, my nose tingled. I could smell something minty and...earthy. Hm.

"Pearl, could you do me a favour, please?" I handed her the note. "A few favours, actually."

CHAPTER NINE

TRYSTAN

I T DIDN'T TAKE LONG to realise that the easiest way into Emerson's office was the front door. A couple showers later, Morgan & Watson's newest clients were standing outside, ready to go meet their lawyer. Or at least, one of their clients was.

"Remember, keep the meeting going as long as possible," I said, straightening my button-down shirt. "If anyone asks, I'm your cousin, here for emotional support."

Bee nodded, dressed head to toe in adorable knitwear that would hopefully inspire some extra sympathy. "Right. My cousin with terrible IBS, who had to run to the bathroom as soon as we arrived and will be with us when he can."

"Stop enjoying this so much. I'll text you when I'm back outside so you can make an excuse and leave. If all goes well, Emerson will never know I was here."

As much as I focused on avoiding Emerson, part of me was still desperate to see him. I couldn't even blame the thoughts on my heat anymore. It was all me.

Getting so close to him would be a risk. If I caught his scent again, I'd have a hard time resisting the pull of his alpha against my omega. Luckily, I'd stocked up on pheromone suppressants.

I just needed to get through this job. Once it was over, it would be easier to stay away from him, and my attraction would fade, like with anyone else. The thought made my chest ache, but it was for the best. There wasn't space for an alpha in my life.

We entered the building and immediately split up. Bee headed for the receptionist's desk, while I weaved through groups of lawyers until I slid into a bathroom stall. It took a few minutes longer than expected—Emerson must've been running late—but eventually, Bee's "affirmative" text came through. Three toilet emojis. Classy.

I waited a couple extra minutes, until I was sure no one else remained in the bathroom, before leaving and heading to the elevator. There were security cameras everywhere. It had taken practice to walk around with my head angled away from cameras in a way that the people around wouldn't see me as acting strange, but it was more than worth it during jobs like this. Following Bee's cryptic emoji message, I took the elevator to the third floor and began searching for Emerson's office.

It was never easy looking for a particular room when I hadn't had the time to properly scope out the building or get a good disguise together, but luck seemed to be on my side today. Down the hallway of the first corner I turned, I hit the jackpot.

An empty assistant's desk outside an equally abandoned office belonging to Emerson Richter. Not wasting any time, I tried the handle—empty *and* unlocked, what a day—and slipped inside, flicking the lock behind me.

Emerson's office was laid out in an almost perfect replica of his home office, albeit a few feet smaller. He'd decorated the walls with more art in place of the additional bookcases he kept at home, but otherwise, the layout was the same.

I wonder what else is similar.

Kneeling behind his desk, I grinned at the sight of a locked drawer. This time, I had no intention of waiting to get it open.

Two pins and a few well-practised twists later, I found...an empty drawer?

"I didn't expect to see you back on your knees so soon, Trystan."

I froze at the sound of his voice, mentally praying it was only my imagination. Carefully glancing over the top of the desk, I spotted Emerson leaning against the open doorframe, keys dangling from one finger as he stared me down. He wore an amused smirk, so different from the first time he found me like this, yet my heart pounded all the same.

I cocked a brow. "Don't s'pose you'll believe I got lost on my way to the bathroom?"

"Afraid not, love." He chuckled as he closed the door behind him and locked it.

Rising to my feet, I tried to appear nonchalant as I leaned against the back of Emerson's leather desk chair. "'Love', hmm. When did we start with pet names?"

"Somewhere between asking for your name and discovering your second break-in."

I looked around the room theatrically, gesturing wildly with my arms to distract from my eyes searching for another way out of the room. "I don't see anything broken here, do you?"

The office only had one door, typical, but no less disappointing. Even a bathroom would have given me options. How the hell was I supposed to get past him without alerting the entire building? Just needed to keep him talking and buy myself time to figure something out.

My fake grin faltered when a photograph poking out of a manila folder on the desk caught my eye. "Oh, but someone's been doing his homework. Never been popular enough to have a stalker before."

"I like to know who I'm dealing with. You left before we could talk properly last time." He took a few steps closer but stayed between the desk and the door. "It's not here, you know."

"Figured that out." My jaw ticked as I cast my eyes over the desk again. "Do you genuinely not use that drawer, or did you empty it especially to tease me?"

"I know far more enjoyable ways to tease you."

"That you do. Won't work, though." I smirked at Emerson's confusion. His brow furrowed in a way that seemed foreign to him. "I'm back on suppressants. Took extras this time, too. Your scent won't affect me again."

Emerson laughed. Not in a mocking way, like he knew something I didn't, but like he found what I'd said genuinely funny. I'd seen people stoned out of their minds laugh less than him. Fucker.

He rested a large hand on his chest as his laughter diffused into chuckles, then turned a charming smile on me. "Do you seriously think that some back-alley drug will stop you from being affected by my scent? I thought you were smarter than this, love."

"I have no sense of smell. At all." I shrugged my shoulders. "Hard to be affected by something you can't sense."

"You think so? Well then, let's test that theory. Come here." He held up his hands before clasping them behind his back. "I won't touch you. Won't do anything you don't ask for."

I hesitated for a heartbeat, then stepped around the desk and slowly approached him. He had to be bluffing, right? My heat was over, so there was no reason for them not to work—even my cheap ones. Suppressants worked on people's pheromones. It was biology. There was no way some alpha scent bullshit would have any... effect on...

Patchouli wafted over me. Sweet, musky earth with spices and a wave of vanilla, gently warming me from my chest. Soothing, with a tingling excitement that promised so much more.

Emerson didn't laugh at my realisation. Instead, he took the final step towards me, close enough now that our lips would touch if I leaned in even slightly.

"Listen well, love. I am your scent match. Do you know what that means?"

I stepped back, my mind struggling to hold on to a thought.

Like a magnet drawn in by my presence, Emerson stepped towards me again, his eyes fixed on mine. Though his hands remained behind him, he was no less intimidating. "It means I am your alpha. Your alpha, chosen by the very core of who you are and by fate itself."

For each step back I took, unable to tear my eyes away from him, he followed until my back hit a wall. He stayed the tiniest distance away, not quite touching me, but close enough that the heat radiating from his body felt like I was standing on the edge of a volcano.

"Therefore, your suppressants won't work with me. I've had your scent and you, mine. We may not have claimed each other fully yet, but your body will not allow you to block out your alpha. I scented your icy aura and the layers of steel, smoke, and earth beneath it the moment you were in the building. You, my omega, cannot hide from me. Not when you're the one person I crave beyond measure."

My resistance melted under his intense gaze, like an ice cube thrown into the earth's core.

"Please, touch me." I spoke against his lips before kissing him like I was drowning and he was the air.

My hands fisted his hair, tugging at the short strands to keep him fused to my face. Hands roamed over my waist and under my thighs. I lifted my leg, wrapping it around his hip as he pressed me firmly against the wall, grinding our hardening cocks against each other through our trousers. Teeth nipped at my lips, and I opened for him, allowing his tongue to enter my mouth as I savoured the taste of my alpha. Every lick of his tongue against my own fuelled my need for him until I knew what I wanted.

Pushing against his chest enough to get some wiggle room between his muscular body and the wall, I dropped to my knees.

His hands automatically moved to stroke my hair. "What are you—"

I cut him off with a long, slow lick over the sizable tent in his trousers as my fingers worked his belt open. He quickly caught onto my idea and shucked his trousers down enough to pull his cock out of his briefs and guide it towards my eagerly waiting mouth.

Sticking out my tongue, I enjoyed the sensation of it entering my mouth. Hot, thick, and heavy. Closing my lips around the head, I swirled my tongue around while sucking gently. A deep moan slipped from Emerson. Salty droplets of flavour burst on my tongue, and I continued to lap them up and take him deeper, coating him in my saliva.

Every gasp and moan I coaxed out of Emerson spurred me on. I wanted to please him. Taste him. Consume him. Feel a powerful alpha come undone from only my mouth.

I took him deeper, bobbing my head further down his cock each time. He hit the back of my throat, and the fingers in my hair tightened. I gagged around him, and sparks of pleasure shot from my scalp to my throbbing erection, but I forced myself to ignore it as Emerson's hips began moving in shallow thrusts.

Tears formed in the corners of my eyes, but I took every thrust of his hips like it was all that kept me alive. He groaned my name, and my hands gripped Emerson's hips. Small crescent marks welled with blood as my nails dug into his skin, but I didn't tap out. I wanted to feel every inch of him until I couldn't take any more.

As black spots dotted my vision, Emerson pulled out enough for me to suck in a breath, then held my hair tight to prevent me from going back down.

"No. Please," I croaked through my abused throat. "I want you to come in my mouth."

Kneeling, he licked away a tear rolling down my cheek and planted a gentle kiss on my temple. "I will, love. But I need you on my desk now, okay?"

I nodded, moving with Emerson as he positioned me on the desk, lying on my back with my head dropping off the side. My mind was a blur, but it felt so different from my heat. Before, my inner omega was the one calling the shots. I'd focused purely on what would make the burning pain in my core stop, and Emerson had been the answer to that.

This time, I was in the driver's seat. And my desires were all my own.

Leaning over me from the side, Emerson unbuttoned my shirt, his eyes fixed on my chest as he slowly unveiled it. Once fully opened, he stroked a large hand over my abdomen. The heat of his palm soaked into my skin, teasing me as I watched him circle around the desk to stand by my head. He tapped his cock against my lips once, twice, and I opened wide for him.

Sucking him from this new angle allowed me to take more of him into my throat so much easier. He pushed in slowly, letting me feel every inch of him as I held onto his hips and ran my tongue over his shaft. I moaned around him as his hands explored my chest, tweaking my piercings like they were his new favourite toys.

"You feel so good, Trystan. Your throat is so perfect."

I wiggled my hips in a pathetic attempt to get some friction in my trousers. How the hell did people wear these every day? Emerson's hands slowly meandered down to my waistband, teasing me with his fingers dipping beneath my belt before stroking back up to pinch my nipples.

Just as I was about to complain, I felt a tongue lick down from my navel and hands freeing my throbbing cock. I groaned as Emerson gripped me, my throat vibrating around his cock. His spare hand circled my neck, his thumb tracing where his cock steadily pumped in and out. I wondered if he could feel himself in my throat. I'd never felt so used and yet so powerful.

My hips bucked into Emerson's hand as he spread my precum with his thumb and moved down to lightly squeeze my balls. I just needed a little bit more. I was so unbelievably close.

"Don't you dare come yet, Trystan," he warned, gripping me firmly at the base, then chuckled as I whined around a mouthful of cock. "That's it, love, wait for me. You're doing so well."

The praise made it even harder to hold back, but I was determined. Digging my fingertips into Emerson's hips, I put all my focus into licking and sucking his soul out through his cock. Every gasp and grunt that reached my ears spurred me on.

Finally, Emerson leaned back slightly. He took his hand from my neck and closed it over the base of his cock, where his knot would inflate, and pumped himself against my lips.

"Ready, love?" he panted, stroking me in time with him. "Come for me now."

Emerson leaned forward, sealing his lips over my cock and sucking hard. My orgasm crashed through me in a speeding wave of bliss. His cum filled my mouth, dribbling from the corner of my lips as I tried to swallow it down. As I coughed through it, Emerson helped me sit up on his desk and pulled me back to lean against him. His arms wrapped around me tightly, and I realised how badly his legs were shaking.

Fuck yeah. I did that.

As we both slowly came back down to earth, we turned to look at each other in the embrace, our breath mingling. Between the tears and cum splattering my face, I surely looked a mess. But the way Emerson stared at me, with a tired half smile and flushed cheeks, was almost like he was admiring me. Closing the gap between us, he licked a dribble of the cum on my chin and kissed it into my mouth. Our tastes mixed together, and I couldn't get enough of the flavour.

A *beep-beep* from his watch snapped us out of the moment, and I hopped off the desk, wordlessly buttoning up my shirt. What the hell was I supposed to say to him now?

Thanks for letting me suck your cock. Could you turn around and let me search the place so I can keep my kneecaps now? Cheers!

As I scrubbed a hand over my face and finished getting myself together, Emerson—equally put together—opened his office door and crooked a finger towards me. I walked to him without thinking, only realising once I was in the hallway. Thankfully, it was empty, except for one guy in a badly fitting suit holding a bunch of folders a little way down the hall.

His hand rested on my hip. "Go back to mine and wait for me there, okay?"

I opened my mouth to argue, but he quickly cut me off, speaking in a low tone.

"I know why you came here today, and we're going to talk about it," he explained. "But not here."

"Ugh, fine." I held out my hand, palm up.

69

Emerson's eyes narrowed, and he took my hand in his. He studied it for a moment, like I was going to trick him, before gently turning it and kissing my knuckles.

My face flushed as I yanked my hand back. "What the hell are you doing? No, give me your key, ass. In case you forgot, I lost mine."

He chuckled, pulling me close by the waist and planting a kiss against my temple. "You're a thief. I'm sure you'll figure something out."

Chapter Ten

Emerson

Nothing was broken when I got home, and I honestly wasn't sure whether that was a good thing.

I wandered through the penthouse, looking for anything out of place, but came up empty. Did Trystan even come? I supposed it was a lot to ask, but I'd still hoped he'd be here.

Mint wafted from my bedroom, and I followed my feet there automatically. Despite cleaning up after his heat, a lot of his scent had permeated the room—both a blessing for memories and a curse for trying to get to sleep. Maybe a nap would be a good idea. It wasn't in my usual routine, but my body clearly needed it.

Strange. The bedroom door was closed. I normally left it open while I was out. It wasn't like anyone went in there except for me.

Turning the handle slowly, I silently opened the door a crack and grinned when the full intensity of Trystan's vetiver scent washed over me. I opened it fully, and my eyes locked on the omega-sized lump in the bed surrounded by pillows.

Approaching silently, I kicked my shoes off and sat on the bed next to him, desperately trying not to jostle him awake. Satisfied he was still asleep, I looked down at him and bit my lip, trying not to grin. It was too sweet seeing him so relaxed. His brow had softened without the scowl painting his features. He was always beautiful, but he looked so much lighter. All the stress of his waking hours melted away.

Part of me wanted to talk to him, hold him, but I resisted, grabbing a book from the nightstand instead. His heat barely finished a day ago, and I had him on knees just this morning. Better to let him rest.

Eventually, a sleepy voice spoke up. "Did you really find me in your bed and decide to read a law textbook? I think I'm offended."

I smiled down at him, admiring the way his dark curls stuck up in every direction. "You looked so peaceful. I didn't want to wake you."

"Well... Thanks. I didn't mean to fall asleep here, though." He blinked a few times, steadily becoming more alert. "Your door-guy came up with bags of these cushions. I was gonna hide 'em somewhere, but then I sat down in here for a minute, and I guess I dozed off."

"Under the duvet?"

"It was chilly."

"With the cushions." I smirked, enjoying the blush creeping across Trystan's cheeks. "You were nesting."

"I don't nest!" he snapped, "Not even in heat."

I looked him over again. He'd only added two of the cushions I'd had delivered today, but combined with the pillows that were already in my bed, there was definitely a wall of squishiness surrounding him. "Maybe you don't do it to the degree of typical omegas, but trust me, this cosy little cocoon you built is a nest."

Trystan's face dropped, and he sat up. "This was a mistake."

"Hey, hey!" I grabbed his shoulder, pulling him back before he could get to his feet. "There's nothing wrong with these instincts. You don't need to hide them, especially not from me."

"Why? Because you're my alpha?" He scoffed, flopping back on the pillows and rubbing his eyes with the heels of his hands. "What does that even *mean*? I'm supposed to hand my life over to you on a platter just because you smell nice?"

"You're supposed to let me take care of you, because we were made for each other," I said, gently prying his hands away from his face. "I know you feel it, even without your heat driving you."

The usually quiet intensity of Trystan's vetiver scent turned powerful, smothering the minty and metallic undertones with leathery, smokier notes. It was like his emotions were ready to turn his earthy aroma into a wildfire, unless I was careful.

"Oh, because you know everything about me now, don't you?" he snapped, turning onto his side to face me and casting a glare that would have made a lesser man recoil. "You may have done your homework, but this is only the third time I've met you. I don't even know you!"

"But do you *want* to know me? Because I want to know everything about you." I leaned towards him, brushing a curl away from his face and tracing his jaw with my fingertips. "And so far, I can see I've barely scratched the surface."

Trystan stared up at me with wide green eyes and all I wanted to do was hold him close and ground him. Finally, he spoke, his voice cracking. "What happens when you don't like what you find?"

"What do you mean 'when'? We've already done that. I wasn't exactly thrilled when I found you trying to rob me. Twice." I smiled, hoping to reassure him, even a little. "Therefore, since we've already crossed that bridge, I can tell you what happens is mind-blowing sex. Does that work for you?"

The corner of his mouth quirked up. "I'm not going to roll over for you and be your obedient little omega because of your dick, you know. No matter how much I enjoy it."

"Is that what you think I want? No, I find your fire far too enchanting to try to smother it. I don't want to own you, Trystan. I want to worship you, because as much as you're mine, I am yours. Everything I do now is for you."

His throat bobbed, and he bit his lower lip, but he didn't pull away. "That's some pretty intense stuff for day three."

"Get used to it, love." I curled an arm around him, pulling our bodies flush against each other, albeit with a duvet covering his lower half. "But also, please don't make me wake up cuffed to the bed again. Not unless you plan on sticking around, that is."

Trystan grinned sheepishly, avoiding eye-contact. "Heh, yeah, that seems reasonable."

Nuzzling into the crook of his neck, I swiped my tongue over the skin below his ear before biting down a little harder than necessary. Trystan let out a small yelp, and I soothed the light mark with my tongue, massaging and sucking the area until he moaned deliciously. "Good to hear. Now, stay the night this time? We can talk about the book and everything tomorrow, just...stay?"

One of his hands moved to my hair, stroking and smoothing over my scalp in a way that made me relax against him. It was such a simple thing, but it felt so intimate.

"Mm, fine," he conceded. "But you have to make me breakfast."

"Seems reasonable." I chuckled, stroking my hand up and down his spine. As it gradually moved lower, a growing hardness pressed against my hip. "Enjoying yourself, love?"

Trystan ground his hip up to me, not ashamed in the slightest. "Mm, can't help it. Feels good. And I've been horny as fuck since your office."

Turning my head, I caught his lips in a bruising kiss, pushing him back onto the pillows and climbing between his thighs. He bucked his hips as he moaned into my mouth, desperately seeking friction against my own semi.

"You didn't knot me today," he said between kisses. "I was hoping to get bent over your desk at some point."

"Oh, the blowjob wasn't enough?" I asked with a grin. "You wanted to spend the afternoon arse-up, stuffed full of cock, leaking cum all the way home. Is that it?"

"You make me sound so selfish."

Rolling off him, I quickly undid a few buttons on my shirt and pulled it over my head. Trystan wriggled out of his sinfully tight jeans. Once we were both undressed, I grabbed the lube and crashed my mouth on his. His hands fisted my hair, tugging me close as I cupped his arse cheeks and groaned into his mouth.

Reaching between us, Trystan took both our cocks in his hand, pumping them together, while my fingers spread his cheeks. I felt around his hole, gently probing his entrance. My finger slid in easily to the second knuckle. He was slick enough I could probably stretch him without lube, but I didn't want to take any chances.

Settling between his legs, I coated my fingers in the lube and went to work. Each stroke inside him dragged out perfect little moans and whimpers that had my inner alpha pacing around my mind. The need to claim my omega was powerful, but one I could hold back for now. Trystan wasn't ready for that, not with everything going on around us.

As I stretched him, he said, "It might be a little late to ask, but you're cool with no condom? I mean, I'm clean and all, but you didn't know that when I was in heat and—"

"Relax, love." My fingers brushed his prostate and dragged a low moan from him. Kissing up his neck, I focused on that spot. "I've used a condom with every partner I've been with, except you. Yours is the only hole painted with my cum, because you're mine. I'm not putting anything between us. Now, get on your hands and knees for me."

"Yes, sir." He winked, turning onto his stomach and raising his arse—dripping with slick—in the air like a perfect omega.

Gripping his hips, I lined up at his entrance and pressed against him. I'd barely pushed the head of my cock in an inch before Trystan was wiggling his hips, eager for more.

"Easy, love." I rubbed my thumbs over his hips. "Take it easy. Let me take my time with you."

"Come on," he whined, pushing against my grip. "I'm ready for you."

"Oh?" I chuckled. "Your hole is clinging to me like a virgin, practically choking me. You think you can handle the rest, love? You think you can take a knot?"

"You know I can!" he wailed, trying to wiggle down onto my cock, but my grip held firm. It took every ounce of restraint in my soul not to slam into him, but I was too entranced by watching him come undone. Feeling him clench around the inch of me inside him, knowing there was so much more just waiting to plunge into him.

"Oh, look at you, love. Such a mess when you don't get what you want straight away." I pushed forward slightly, still hardly breaching him even as he pushed back with considerable force. "All right, since you seem so sure. Go ahead." I dropped my hands from his hips. "Fuck yourself on my cock."

For a moment, he didn't move. He just looked at me over his shoulder, biting his lip and coated with a light sheen of sweat. Slowly, he pressed back against me, gasping at the feeling. When I didn't move to stop him, his movements grew bolder. He pushed himself back, further each time, until he was finally fully impaled on my cock.

Low moans and the sound of skin slapping skin filled the room. I should have felt used, watching him slam his hips back against me over and over. With anyone else, I probably would have. But this was Trystan, my omega. In my mind, there was nothing hotter than seeing him chase his own pleasure and take what he needed from me.

I watched my cock disappear into his hole, my hands in tight fists at my side as his cheeks pressed against my hips, before it reemerged, smothered in his slick. He was staking a claim on me, and I loved it. As much as he was mine, I was also his.

"Fuck me. Please, Emerson," he panted. "I'm so close, but I need you to—"

My hips snapped forward before he could finish, driving him into the mattress at a relentless pace. Rolling us onto our sides, I took Trystan's cock in my hand, red and dripping precum, and stroked him with a tight fist.

"That's it, love. You did so well," I breathed, holding him close with my spare arm. "Let me take you the rest of the way."

He could only moan in response as he fisted the sheets. My knot inflated as I pushed it into Trystan once, twice more before it locked us together, then my release shot into him.

Vetiver hit my senses like a shotgun blast as Trystan exploded in my hand, yelling my name like a desperate prayer. I stroked him through his orgasm, milking him of every drop of pleasure as my hips pressed into him until he tiredly slapped my hand away with a worn-out whimper.

"I've got you, love," I said with a shaky breath. "Just sleep for now."

CHAPTER ELEVEN

TRYSTAN

I NEVER SHOULD'VE NAPPED in his bed. But the past few days had finally caught up to me. The bed was there and...it smelled right.

It smelled of *him*.

Even now, a few hours of sleep and another knot later, I felt safe here. Usually, when I stayed the night with a partner, I never got any sleep. My instincts would be screaming at me to get out, run.

I'd never felt so rested, yet my mind refused to calm. I still had a job to do, and Emerson had got in the way of that twice already. I was running out of time.

The alpha in question rumbled behind me. "Go back to sleep, love. I can hear you thinking."

"What? No, you can't," I grumbled into the pillow.

"Calling me a liar? You're mean in the mornings." He chuckled, tightening his arm around my waist as his knot pulsed inside me.

Gasping at the sensation filling me, I pressed back against him. We'd been locked together for the past hour—after I'd woken up needing an early morning dose of alpha—but I still couldn't get enough of feeling this full. It was incredible. Each pulse of his cock triggered waves of pleasure in me. Totally worth being sore for a day.

Eventually, Emerson's knot deflated, and he pulled out of me, kissing up my neck. "I believe I promised you breakfast."

I grinned, carefully rolling over to face him. "You definitely did. I need a shower first, though. You might be the right amount of sweaty to still be lickable, but I think you'd prefer I leak two knots worth of cum in the shower instead of on your bedsheets."

"How thoughtful of you." Emerson chuckled, taking my face in his hands and lightly kissing my lips. "There should be an unopened toothbrush under the sink. Help yourself to whatever you need, and I'll use the guest shower."

"You sure?"

He nodded, running a hand through his hair. "Yeah, I feel like you might want to work up to using the bathtub you were tied up in."

"Aww, look who got on board the thoughtful train."

My arse received a playful warning slap, and I rolled back over to watch the door as Emerson left for the guest bathroom. Fuck, I really hadn't properly appreciated how sexy he was until now.

His waist to shoulders ratio alone was insane. No wonder he'd made me pass out when we first met.

After an awkward run to the bathroom and one of the greatest showers of my life—I could seriously get used to rich-people plumbing—I dressed in yesterday's clothes and headed towards the kitchen. It was strange to feel so at home in Emerson's penthouse when I'd only really spent time in the bedroom and bathrooms. Maybe it was the way his scent naturally filled the space. It was homely, and my inner omega was relaxed here. I didn't feel an innate need to keep my guard up at all times.

Following the sound of sizzling and the smell of fried foods in the air, I found Emerson at the stove, already working on breakfast. It was the most casual I'd ever seen him—except for when he was naked—in sweatpants with a tight white t-shirt and damp hair. Looking at him like this, I wasn't totally sure which I preferred.

Nope. Still preferred naked.

My stomach rumbled loudly, snapping me out of my fantasies and announcing my presence.

Emerson chuckled. "You have a lot of trouble sneaking up on me, don't you?"

"Apparently," I grumbled, leaning around him to admire his cooking. "Wow, you're going all out for breakfast. This a regular thing for you?"

"Usually only on weekends for myself, but for you..." He shrugged. "Whenever you want it."

"Using my stomach to get into my pants is low. Also, for future reference, I prefer pancakes over waffles."

"Noted. I'm nearly done, so sit down. There's orange juice on the counter." Emerson turned to me, looking me up and down curiously. "Did you change out of your office clothes before coming over yesterday?"

"Obviously. I needed a shower after leaving your office. Plus, I hate wearing stuffy shirts like that." I sat on a barstool and took a big gulp of orange juice. "Were you hoping to see me dressed in your clothes or something?"

A light blush crept up his cheeks. Got him. "Definitely not against it. I like our scents mixing. It's relaxing, somehow. Know what I mean?"

"Sort of," I lied, strangely annoyed that we'd had the same thought process. "It's been years since I've experienced scents and stuff, so it's kind of new to me right now." I took another sip of juice and made a mental note to take a suppressant after eating. There were a few stashed in my wallet for emergencies. "Bee nearly talked me out of coming here, actually. They did say you were very professional for the ten minutes you bothered to sit in the meeting with them, though."

Emerson cast me a side-eyed glance before turning his attention back to the eggs. "I decided that my colleague would be more appropriate for the case they brought to us."

"Mhmm. Sure." I nodded with mock-understanding. "And I'm sure that thought had nothing to do with someone creeping around your office at the time?"

"Of course not. I'm a professional." He waved away the accusation with a spatula. "It was mere coincidence that leaving your friend in my colleague's capable hands allowed me the opportunity to return to other pressing matters."

"You're such a lawyer."

Reaching into the cupboards, Emerson started pulling out plates and cutlery. "Speaking of, do you want to discuss the elephant in the room while we eat or after?"

I shrugged. May as well get it over with. "Why wait? At least if we're eating, you can't seduce me for information again."

His lips quirked in a half smirk as he plated the food. "You have such little faith in me."

Not true. I knew, deep down, that if anyone could make a full English breakfast sexy enough for me to start spilling secrets, it was Emerson. But the longer I denied it, the longer I could avoid it.

Once he sat next to me, Emerson didn't waste time getting started. "You said before that you never meet your clients, but I assume you're aware of the case your target relates to, yes?"

"I know enough to find my target, but I never look up extra details. It makes it easier to get the job done without getting distracted."

"Makes it easier to work for criminals, you mean?"

84

My jaw ticked. "I know you don't approve, but has it ever occurred to you that I enjoy what I do?"

He raised an eyebrow. "Stealing?"

"Sneaking in unseen, or better yet, in plain fucking sight," I explained, sitting back in my chair. "Getting what my client wants without anyone knowing I was ever there. Every job is its own puzzle that I have to solve."

A grin spread across my face, and I thought back to when I first started thieving as a kid. A dare that turned into a hobby, then a method of survival. But even through those transitions, I still felt the same rush with each job.

Emerson watched me with a sad half smile. I wasn't sure exactly how much Emerson knew of my past, but I, at least, wanted him to know who I was in the present, even if he didn't approve of it.

After a moment, I added, "Not to mention I'm really good at it."

He chuckled, lightening the mood. "I'm sure you are, despite the string of bad luck recently."

"I put that down to a particularly annoying target rather than an issue of my own skill."

"Spoken like a lawyer."

We ate in silence for a minute. I don't think either of us really wanted to have this conversation. But it wasn't long until not even bacon could distract me from the tension anymore.

"I know I don't have a moral leg to stand on, Emerson. It just isn't as simple as good and bad—"

"Miranda Fisher *sold omegas*." Emerson stared me down, the intensity of his eyes burning into me. "The diary you've been attempting to steal is evidence in the case against her, further proof of where she planned to meet and deal in human lives. For fuck's sake, Trystan, if you hadn't been hiding your status, you..."

"I'd be one of her victims," I finished for him, my jaw clenching. "Why do you think I've been taking suppressants for over a decade? I'm well aware of the dangers my status brings."

He turned on the barstool to face me and placed a hand on my knee, squeezing gently. "So work with me to bring whoever hired you to justice."

I shook my head. "My hands are tied here, Emerson. I can probably buy you an extra day or two with the diary, if that'll help your case, but I need you to stay out of my way. This is something I have to do."

He scoffed. "Even though you know you can do something to help?"

"It wouldn't do any good!" I ran a hand through my hair, pulling at the strands before huffing out a breath. "One way or another, that book will be delivered to my client. If I'm not the one to retrieve it for them, that'll mean Roman doesn't have a use for me anymore."

Emerson stared at me with fierce determination in his pale eyes, his hand holding my knee like a lifeline. "I can keep you safe, Trystan. You have to trust me."

I almost believed him. The worst part was that I desperately wanted to do just that. I ached to lean into my omega instincts and depend on my alpha. Let him take control of the situation and do what was best for me. Be the one who was protected for a change.

Instead, I was trapped. Forced to make the worst decision, knowing what it would do. The decision that would prove him right about me and make him hate me. Still, it was the choice that would keep us both breathing at the end of it. That had to be worth something.

Chapter Twelve

Emerson

It felt wrong leaving Trystan to come into the office today, like a piece of me was missing. Each time I saw him, the urge to hold on to him grew stronger. It was supposed to be easy. After all, it was in our nature.

Instead, I pissed him off. All I wanted to do was to keep him safe, hold him in my arms, and breathe in that wild vetiver scent while his curls tickled my nose. He'd been opening up to me, showing me the sides of him he'd kept hidden from everyone for years. But he was so entrenched in the lawless world he grew up in. Did he even know how to let someone help?

Did he even want to get out of it?

Luckily for me, Trystan made one crucial error during our conversation. I wasn't sure he'd realised he said it. Maybe part of him was unconsciously trusting of me, or it was an error in the heat of the moment. Regardless, I fully intend to exploit that mistake for everything it was worth, whether he liked it or not.

Roman.

It wasn't much to go on, but there was no mistaking the fear in Trystan's eyes when he said that name. Tension had immediately coiled in my chest, my alpha screaming at me to get more information, but I knew pushing my omega at that point would've only made things worse. Better he not realise what little information he gave me, than close off completely.

At least I had a chance now.

"Hey, are you done working on that diary thing yet?" Harris asked, barging into my office with a panicked Pearl trailing behind him.

I waved to her to say it was okay. It wasn't, but it also wasn't her fault that my friend had the audacity of a cat that insisted on staring you down while you were on the toilet. Times like this, I really missed my home office.

Closing my laptop, I leaned back in my chair. "No, I'm still working on it. Had a few things come up that've extended the timeline." *A robbery. Two of them, actually.* "Why do you ask?"

Harris shrugged, looking over my bookcase of pending cases. "Just curious if you'd found anything or not. Rhodes said it was a longshot finding any new information, right?"

"When did you become such a pessimist?"

"Since it started taking up all of your time and keeping you out of the courtroom." He rolled his eyes. "You should delegate some of the evidence research so you can spend more time doing the work that matters."

"And who do you suggest I delegate to?" I asked, wondering where this was going. He usually called my need to personally review evidence a waste of time. "This sort of thing is above Pearl's remit."

Harris scratched the back of his neck. "I mean, I've got my own cases, but I could help the big dogs out once in a while. I've read up on the Fisher case, so I know what to look for."

This was a first for Harris. True, he worked hard, but I'd never seen him seek additional responsibilities or offer his help on tasks he didn't deem a priority.

Before I could politely decline, the intercom buzzed on my desk, and Pearl's voice filtered through. "Ms Watson is here to speak with you. She says it's urgent."

Harris jumped at Pearl's words, immediately heading for the door. "Better get going. Don't want the boss lady to catch me slacking. Let me know about looking at the diary! I've got time!"

The door opened, revealing Norah leaning against the doorframe with arms folded across her chest. "What was that, Harris? I have plenty of cases waiting if you're looking for work."

I laughed from my desk. "Stop torturing him, Norah. He was trying to be helpful."

"Well, that makes a change." She narrowed her dark eyes as Harris edged past her, shutting the door behind her as soon as he was barely over the threshold. "Still don't know why Frankie hired him."

"You're too hard on him."

"And you're not my boss." Norah shook her head. "I've given him plenty of chances. Something about him doesn't sit right with me. Anyway, that's not what I'm here to talk about. My stolen tech case is falling apart, and I need some good news. Please tell me you're getting somewhere with this diary."

I stood from my desk, motioning to the sofa against the wall. "I'm getting through it. What's wrong with the tech case?"

Norah groaned, flopping back on my sofa and covering her face with one arm. "There's no evidence. Police say there's no one at the company willing to talk, and they can't get a warrant without something more to go on. Right now, it's my client's word against theirs, and the police aren't willing to 'waste resources on her'. Actual quote."

Taking a seat beside her, I asked, "Is there anyone else you can get to look into it?"

"I've asked everyone I can, and they all said the same thing: not enough grounds for a warrant." She pulled her hair out of the chignon she wore for in-person meetings and sighed in relief, then relaxed back into the sofa and forced a smile. "I came here for some joy, Emerson. Tell me about your omega. How are things going? Have you claimed him yet?"

"No, not yet." I slouched back, already exhausted by the memory of this morning. "Things are tense. There's an ongoing issue with his job."

She smiled sadly. "I take it you don't approve of whatever he does."

"Understatement of the century." I chuckled.

"Ugh, he's not another lawyer, is he? I'm convinced we're the worst people to live with. Oh, no, wait! A P.I.?" She gasped, slapping the sofa in a fit of either rage or excitement. It was hard to tell. "I dated one of those nosy pricks before marrying Frankie! He was constantly sneaking around, the suspicious arse. And that was when he could be bothered to come home."

This must have been before I met her. Norah and her husband—the other partner at our firm—only married three years ago, but they'd been together as long as I'd known them. It was rare to see a pair of alphas as compatible as they were.

Norah took a breath from her tirade. "Oh, I'm sorry. I didn't mean to make this about me." Scooching closer, she took my hand and gave it a gentle squeeze. It wasn't a romantic gesture, merely familiar. She was the closest person I could call family without hours of travelling. "Look, it's never easy when the alpha in you makes the choices but have faith in your instincts. They led you to your omega. You'll figure it out together."

"Thank you, Norah. Honestly, I'm surprised you and Frankie haven't found a suitable omega."

"We've stopped looking," she admitted, laughing as I gaped at her. "Don't look so shocked. Our alpha marriage works for us."

I held up my hands, quickly snapping myself out of my surprise. "Sorry, sorry. I've just never known either of you to give up on anything."

"It's not giving up. We're just happy appreciating what we have." Norah smiled widely, and I immediately believed every word she said. She seemed genuinely happy in her marriage. It gave me hope that even unconventional arrangements could work out. "That said, if we happen to magically stumble upon the perfect omega, willing to take on us both, I'd take the plunge in a heartbeat."

I grinned, unable to resist asking, "Even if they were a P.I.?"

Laughter bubbled out of her. "Yep, even then. And I know Frankie would say the same."

Norah's casual confidence eased the tension in my chest. She was right. I needed to trust my instincts with Trystan. He may be too deep into his situation with Roman to find a way out alone, but I could clearly see a future with him. There were ways he could use his unique skills where he wouldn't end up in jail. Trystan was smart, stealthy, and fiercely determined—traits that made him irresistible to me while also driving me completely insane.

We would make our match work. I just had to convince him to try.

As I tapped my fingers on the arm of the sofa, an idea struck me. Grinning at my friend, I asked, "Could you excuse me while I make a call? I have an idea that could help your tech case."

Once I was alone again, I dialled the newest number in my phone.

Come on. Pick up...

Just as I was ready to record a voicemail, Trystan's voice grumbled through the speaker, "Emerson? When did you add your number to my phone?"

Oops. Probably should've told him that earlier. "While you were in the shower. But that's not important right now."

He groaned but didn't hang up. I wasn't sure whether it was instinct or curiosity keeping him on the line, but I was grateful either way. "You better not be calling for phone sex or something after this morning."

"Actually, Mr Wells, I'm calling strictly on business."

Chapter Thirteen

Trystan

"**R**emind me why the fuck you agreed to this?" Bee snarked from behind their laptop.

We'd set up near the window of a busy coffee shop, across the street from the Rose and Swan pub. It gave me the perfect vantage point to look out for where my target was expected to be heading for a cheeky after-work drink any minute now. From Bee's research, they had a very productive Monday, and this would be the perfect time to strike.

"It's an easy job," I explained, relaxing in my chair enough to appear content, while I watched the pub's entrance like a hawk.

Bee took a bite of a flaky pastry, crumbs flying as they spoke, "Uh-huh. You're not swaying that lawyer over to the dark side with this move, you know."

"I'm not trying to," I said a little too quickly. "He asked for a favour, and I have the time to help him out, is all."

"Only because you've been avoiding your actual job." The words were harsh, but Bee's eyes were full of concern. "I get needing to rest over the weekend, but it's almost been a week since you first tried—"

"It's *fine*. I've got a few more days until the deadline." At least, I hoped I did.

Roman's client still said the diary was at Emerson's office. All I needed to do was buy Emerson enough time to get what he needed from it and then steal it before it went back into police custody. Easy peasy. Everybody won. Well, the people important to me won.

When did I start thinking of Emerson as someone important to me? Ugh, this scent match crap was messing with my head. I'd managed to stay away from him since leaving his penthouse Friday morning, but deep down, I was itching to see him again. My mind kept playing scenarios of how I could "accidentally" bump into him again, like I had some schoolyard crush. Fucking embarrassing.

Things just felt better around him. I felt more like myself, even when I had to defend my morally questionable career. Being in his presence soothed something inside me, and I missed that feeling. I missed him. The way he challenged me. The way he looked at me like I was the centre of his world when I talked about trying to fucking rob him.

When I closed my eyes, I could still see the look on his face when he insisted he could keep me safe. He genuinely believed it, and I wanted to believe him, too.

Bee passed me a small device from their backpack that looked remarkably similar to a vape pen. "Here, this should record everything you need and send it straight to me here in real time. Even if you fall on your arse and break it, if I've heard the words here, we'll have it saved. Just stick it in your pocket, get in as close as you can, and don't get caught."

I twirled it in my fingers as a blond woman wearing a sharp pantsuit with a distinctive red coat and bag headed into the pub. Exactly as described. Three men in suits followed her closely, laughing and playfully crowding each other—her colleagues.

Perfect. The whole gang's here.

Shoving the device in my jeans pocket, I stood. "Never do."

Bee snorted into their coffee. "Until recently, sure."

It didn't take long to find my targets inside the pub, crowded around a high bar table. Most of the large firms in the area would still have people working late into the evening, but this group was celebrating a big win in technology development. Technology that Norah's client, Claudia, claims they stole from her.

Once I'd grabbed a coke from the bar, I positioned myself at the window, pretending to people-watch with my back to the group I was actually here for. There wasn't anyone between us, so the mic should pick up their conversation clearly. Shooting a text to Bee, I waited for the chaos.

It only took a minute for my phone to *ping*, along with everyone within ten metres of me.

Here we go.

One of the men quickly spoke, his voice rumbling with a deep timber. "Mate, did you seriously just click an unknown link over public Wi-Fi?"

"It's an article about our project," a younger voice replied. "Wait a sec, Georgia! You need to read this. It says they're pulling our funding!"

Georgia scoffed, "What? It has to be fake. We barely closed that deal two hours ago."

Young-voice continued, "It was only posted ten minutes ago. It says that police have launched an investigation into the creation of our tech, prompting an immediate loss of funding from the firm."

The third man finally spoke up. "Crap! It must be Claudia. She said she was going to get a lawyer. But how does the press know already?"

The first voice shushed him. "Shut up. That's impossible."

Young-voice started panicking, "But we were careful. She's got nothing on us! They can't prove we stole anything."

"Keep your fucking voice down, James," Georgia hissed.

I kept the recording going for another twenty minutes, quietly enjoying my drink and scrolling through my phone as the suits behind me collectively crapped their pants. I really didn't think they'd fall for a fake news report that easily, especially one that popped up directly on their phones. What a bunch of fucking idiots. The recording wouldn't be enough for any convictions, but it would get a warrant to search for hard evidence. Either way, my job was done.

Bee and I quickly regrouped at the coffee shop before heading straight to the Morgan & Watson office. Unlike the last time we were here, we stood out like sore thumbs amongst the suits still milling around the reception area. Yet no one stopped us as we made a beeline to the elevator. Good to know that we could stroll right in if we walked with enough purpose.

"You sure you're okay being here?" Bee asked, hitting the button for Emerson's floor.

"Yeah, totally. We're just delivering our side of a contract. Nothing's going to happen this time."

Bee studied me up and down, not at all buying what I was selling. "It's okay if you want to see him, you know."

My eyes flicked to theirs, then quickly away. As much as I appreciated the support, it wasn't okay for me to want my alpha. Not as long as I was under Roman's thumb.

The elevator doors opened, and we silently headed down the corridor to Emerson's office. The floor seemed empty, not unusual for late afternoon, but I suddenly worried I should've called first to say we were coming. Before I could pull my phone out to call Emerson, I spotted a young blond woman sitting at the desk outside his office.

Her head snapped up as we approached, and a pleasant smile spread across her face. "Trystan Wells? My name is Pearl. I'm Mr Richter's assistant. It's nice to meet you." She stood, offering her hand to shake, and I took it. Her hand was smooth and delicate, her nails neatly polished, but she had a firm, confident grip. Must be needed when working around alphas. She turned to Bee. "And you must be—"

"Bee." They leaned forward, shaking her hand enthusiastically. "As in, Bumble."

"Yes, I was sorry to hear our colleagues couldn't provide you the help you sought last week. Especially as Emerson had to see to other matters at the time." Pearl gave me a pointed look, her eyebrows raised with a smirk as she returned to her seat.

Bee either didn't notice the look, or took pity on me for once and didn't say anything about it. "Eh, I knew it was a longshot when I came in."

Pearl gestured to the sofa behind us. "Emerson is in a meeting right now, but please, take a seat. He shouldn't be much longer."

I nodded but stayed standing, bouncing slightly on my toes as a strange, nervous energy sparked through me. My eyes darted around the small waiting area, unable to stay focused on one thing for too long. Bee lounged on the sofa, not a care in the world, while Pearl sat opposite, swiftly tapping keys on her laptop. The sound faded into the background like white noise as my pulse pounded in my ears.

Despite taking my suppressants earlier, Emerson's leather and patchouli scent filtered through the door. Guess that scent match-recognition thing really wasn't going away. Could he already smell that I was here waiting for him?

My eyes flicked to Pearl again, only to find her watching me with interest. Scratching at the back of my neck—when had it got so sweaty?—I asked, "You, uh, like working here?"

Trystan Wells, small-talk extraordinaire.

Taking pity on me, her gaze softened. "Emerson is the best boss I've had. He's a good man and easy to trust."

Pearl's words weren't lost on me, but doubts still clawed at my mind. Emerson may be a good lawyer, one of the best from what I'd heard, but I wouldn't be accepting him as a lawyer. To me, he was an alpha. *My* alpha.

Footsteps snapped my attention as a short, pale man in an expensive, but ill-fitting suit stopped at the end of the hallway. He held a small stack of files as he stared down at me, tilting his head slightly, then focused on Pearl.

Keeping my voice low, so not to be overheard, I asked her, "Do you know that guy?"

She glanced over before rolling her eyes back to her laptop. "Oh, that's Harris. He's harmless."

"You sure? He's staring pretty intensely."

The office door swung open, and Emerson strolled out, laughing with the two people following him. The sound made something flutter in my chest, completely distracting me from the creepy suit. By the time my brain rebooted enough to look back, he was already gone.

"Trystan, perfect timing." Emerson smiled at me, making my stomach do that annoying fluttery thing again. "I'd like you to meet Norah and Francis, the firm's partners and close friends of mine."

A beautiful woman with dark skin and a dazzling smile—Norah, I assumed—offered me her hand. "So good to finally meet you. Emerson has been annoyingly tight-lipped when it comes to you."

I shook her hand, nodding politely before turning my attention to the second stranger.

"Call me Frankie, please," he said, giving my hand a firm shake as he cast his eyes over me. Frankie wasn't as broadly built as Emerson, but he clearly worked out regularly. Enough that I was intimidated just standing beside him, especially as his grip on my hand lingered. "Yes, Emerson, I'm surprised you haven't been bragging about this one. He's definitely something special."

In the blink of an eye, Emerson's expression turned from cheerful to murderous. The warming vanilla in his scent overwhelmed the patchouli, the spice heating the air around us as he snaked an arm behind me. His hand gripped my hip, and he not-so-subtly pulled me away from his boss as he ground out the words, "Well, you can't blame me for wanting to keep him all to myself."

Frankie watched with a smirk spread across his pale, freckled cheeks. Throwing me a wink, he said, "Not at all."

Norah softly *thwapped* her partner's chest. "Stop baiting him, dear. Now, I believe you have something for me, Trystan?"

Hopping up from the sofa, Bee bounced into the centre of the most awkward moment of my life, holding up a memory card. "Hi, yes. I'm Bee, and I'd love to get out of here before one of these two starts pissing on my flatmate's leg."

She chuckled, carefully plucking the memory card from Bee's fingers. "I like you, Bee. I assume everything we need is on here?"

They nodded. "Any issues, you all know how to get in touch with Trys. I'll send an invoice for our services."

"Thank you both," she said sincerely. "Not only have you potentially saved my case with this, but you may have saved a promising young woman's career. I don't usually like using private investigators, but in this case, I'm extremely grateful."

My body tensed at Norah's words, and Emerson's grip on my hip tightened. *Private investigators? News to me.*

While Bee basked in the praise of a job well done, my alpha leaned in closely to murmur low in my ear, "My office, now."

With a territorial squeeze of my hip, Emerson guided me towards his office, never once breaking contact with me. Bee and I shared a quick look as I walked past them. Their eyebrows raised in question, and I flicked them an *okay* hand sign with my thumb and index finger. I could handle my alpha. The real question was whether he could handle me.

The door closed behind us, and Emerson's mouth crashed against mine. His lips devoured me like he was trying to own the deepest essence of me. I could only cling to his shoulders, digging my fingers into the muscles as our bodies pressed together. It felt so good to be near him again, to touch him again. My inner omega had craved his comfort, but I still needed more. I needed him to claim me.

Emerson spoke against my lips between his kisses. "I missed you the last few days. It's hard staying away, even when I want to give you space."

"One weekend was your idea of space?"

"I thought you needed it after our talk the other morning."

He leaned in to kiss me again, and I bit his lip hard, but not hard enough to draw blood. He flinched.

"So you decided to tell them I'm a private investigator. That's the angle you're playing?"

Emerson traced his thumb over my jawline, staring deep into my eyes. "There's no angle, love."

I bit the inside of my cheek and studied his face, searching for any trace of a lie. He seemed honest. He believed what he was saying, but it didn't make sense to me. Shaking my head out of his grip, I asked, "Then what the fuck are you trying to do here, Emerson? This shit isn't my world."

He didn't let me step away, holding me against him with his arm around my back. The body heat coming off him felt like a brand, even through our clothes. "Only because you don't *think* it can be your world. But I know we can have a future, Trystan. All you need to do is listen to me."

I rolled my eyes, growling, "Again, with the alpha bullshit!"

"I know what you need!"

"No! I don't know if this is some sad attempt to save me or fix me, but either way, *stop it*," I snapped, finally pushing him away with both hands on his chest. "I'm not some fuckable project for a lonely alpha, and I don't want your help!"

Emerson's pale eyes widened, and he reached a hand out to me. "Trystan, you're not—"

"I can't trust you."

Worse, I wasn't sure I even wanted to try.

Chapter Fourteen

Emerson

THE SILENCE IN MY office was deafening. I didn't even try to stop Trystan from storming out, and now...

As a lawyer, I cannot work for a client unless they trust me to do what's right on their behalf. It's a lot of faith to put in someone, but I'd never, not once, failed to gain their trust.

So then why, with the most important person finally brought into my life, would I fail so terribly?

I'd only wanted Trystan to see that he had options in life. He didn't need to be constantly looking over his shoulder, waiting for the law to catch up with him, or worse.

Maybe I should've waited until we'd dealt with his employer first, but I couldn't help it. Every day in the week since he broke into my life had left me wanting more of him. My inner alpha ached to claim my omega. As far as that side of me was concerned, we had already waited long enough to start our future.

Our life together would be unconventional, but that thought only excited me more. Trystan brought an exhilarating energy with him whenever we met, brightening my world in every way. He was an entire spectrum of colours in a world of shadowy ink that threatened to consume me once again now that he was gone.

A gentle knock dragged me away from my thoughts and out of the cage of my office. Pearl waited in the bright hallway, not in her usual corporate attire, but in leggings and a baggy sweater, her hair piled on top of her head in a bright scrunchie.

"Sorry to interrupt. I didn't want to leave without giving you this in person." She handed me a plain folder. "It's the details of that license plate you asked me to look up a few days ago. It's registered under a false name, but I've finally managed to connect it to someone."

"Thank you, but it's getting late. Why are you still here?"

Pearl waved a hand in the air, brushing away the question like no big deal. "Oh, Harris asked for a favour, and I felt bad refusing. Plus, you were still here, and I wanted to give you some time before bringing this to you. I'm going in a moment, though. Gym, then home."

A weak smile pulled at my cheeks. She worked far too hard. "Next time, please tell him 'no'. Or I'll talk to him. You're usually here late enough as is."

"It was no trouble, really."

"Well, I appreciate it. I'll look it over at home."

Hefting her bag onto her shoulder, Pearl looked at me, raising a blonde eyebrow. "You're not seeing Trystan tonight?"

My shoulders sank, and I shook my head silently. None of my plans for the night involved seeing my omega. It made me want to scream until my throat bled.

"I saw the look on his face as he left," Pearl admitted, grabbing my full attention. "Personally, if I looked like that, I wouldn't want my alpha to leave me alone for very long."

Meeting her eyes, I asked, "Even if your alpha was the problem?"

"Especially then."

She had a point. Every instinct in my body was telling me to go after him, to find some way of making him understand. I hated giving him space when I thought it would help. Maybe it was time to lean more on my alpha side.

Standing a bit straighter, I waved the folder, playfully shooing her towards the elevator. "Go. Take care getting home. I'll see you tomorrow."

Pearl smiled, seemingly satisfied with the change in my demeanour. "Okey-dokey. It's been nice having you in the office more, by the way."

"Don't push it."

Trystan's apartment building was not what I'd call homely. Admittedly, I chose my place based purely on aesthetics and security—though, apparently, the latter needed work—but this was in a league of its own. A much dirtier, smellier league.

Yet for a chance with my omega, I'd live here forever without a single regret.

Not trusting the elevator, I climbed up the stairs to the third floor and found Trystan's front door. My hand hovered near the wood as I inhaled deeply.

There. That faint hint of mint in the air.

I'm home.

The door opened before I could knock, revealing my omega in nothing but sweatpants hanging low on his hips. His chest heaved as he stared at me, his emerald eyes wide.

"It's you. I could actually smell you out here. Wait, how are you here?"

"Bee put this address on the forms when you both visited last week." I held up a paper bag of takeout containers like an offering. "Mind if I come in?"

He hesitantly took the bag and stepped aside. Thankfully, the inside of his flat was a lot cleaner than the outside. The living room and kitchen were one room, likely advertised as an open plan, but the reality was a lot more cramped. A fairly large sofa sat facing a TV, but most of the room was taken up by an impressive corner desk with a computer and multiple monitors.

Apparently, Trystan's flatmate preferred the work-from-home lifestyle as well.

Peering inside the bag while he kicked the door closed, Trystan asked, "What are these? Waffles?"

"Pancakes," I answered, casting my eyes around the room. "You said you preferred them, right?"

"Yeah, that's right." The corner of his mouth twitched in the tiniest hint of a smile. "Mind if I save them for breakfast? I already ate."

"Of course. I came here to talk about what happened earlier."

Leaving the bag on the kitchen counter, he took a seat on the sofa, curling his legs under him in the corner. "Talk or apologise? Because I know which I'm more likely to listen to."

"Hopefully a healthy mix of both." Sitting beside him, I asked, "You've never had an alpha in your life, have you?"

Trystan shook his head, tapping his fingers against his knee. "Even my parents were betas. Turns out you don't need to be an alpha to hate your omega son." He laughed bitterly. I was so glad they were dead. "But yeah, I've always stayed away from alphas where I could...until recently."

"That makes sense. If you don't mind me asking, when was your last heat before we met?"

"I don't know. Guessing maybe...a year ago?"

A low, disapproving growl rumbled out of me, and I took his hand in mine, squeezing gently. "You're supposed to take breaks from suppressants every few months to have your heat."

"I'm also supposed to be an upstanding citizen. Look how well that's going." He chuckled, genuine humour lighting his beautiful eyes. "Why all the questions? This isn't how I thought this conversation would go."

"You don't look after yourself," I stated simply. "In the short time I've known you, you've constantly denied your needs as an omega, and frankly, it's put you in some rough situations."

"If telling me how badly I run my life is your way of apologising, you're doing great."

"An alpha's job is to care for their mate. You've had to hide and deny who you are for so long, I think acceptance scares you. That it'll somehow strip you of who you are. Am I close?"

"You better have a point soon," he gritted out through a tightly clenched jaw.

"I'll take that as a 'yes,'" I muttered, rubbing a thumb back and forth over his knuckles. "Trystan, I don't want you because you're an omega. I want you because you're *mine*, just as much as I am yours. If you were a beta or another alpha, or even if I was an omega, it wouldn't change anything for me."

Trystan's throat bobbed as I spoke, but he stayed silent. The only indication that he was listening was his hand slowly squeezing mine a little harder with each word.

"I never intended to try changing who you are. My only goal is to keep you safe, which you don't make easy, by the way."

Laughter bubbled out of him for a moment, along with a tear he could no longer hold back. He still refused to look at me. I

111

reached up with the hand holding onto him and circled my arm around him, pulling him close. He didn't fight me. Didn't yell or glare. He just curled into me, resting his head on my shoulder and allowing me to hold him.

Vetiver continued to emanate from him as his soft curls tickled my jaw. Each inhale of his essence expanded throughout my chest, relaxing my shoulders and solidifying my resolve.

"Even if you reject me as your alpha, I'll continue to protect you in any way that I can for as long as I am on this earth," I promised, pressing my lips against his temple, then leaned close to look into his teary green eyes. "It's okay if you decide you don't want this, but it won't change the fact that I am yours and you are mine. My omega. My mate. I'm all in if you'll accept me."

Tension lingered in the air, thick and constricting around my throat as I waited for Trystan to say something. Anything. *Please.*

His hand released mine, and for a moment, all I could feel was the cool, empty air where he used to be. Relief surged through my veins as warmth enveloped my thighs, and a weight settled on me. Long fingers slid through my hair, gripping the strands to tilt my head and forcing me to gaze up at the omega straddling me.

He leaned down to me, his lips hovering a hair's breadth above mine. "You won't be able to bribe your way into my flat with pancakes every time you piss me off, you know."

"Won't need to. I'm never letting you walk away from me again."

Running my hands up his thighs, I held his hips, my heart pounding as I patiently waited for him to make the first move. The moment he closed the miniscule gap between us, my chest swelled, and my alpha roared triumphantly. Our mouths moved in tandem, tasting and memorising each other more with each addictive movement.

"This really wasn't how I thought the conversation would go." Trystan chuckled breathlessly. "I half-expected you'd throw me over your shoulder, slap me on the arse, and tell me not to run off again."

"I'd be happy to do that if it'd make you feel better."

He purred in my lap, every bit the content omega as he peppered soft kisses across my jaw and down to my collar. Pausing for a moment, he breathed against my skin, inhaling my scent and steadily relaxing against me.

"I'm still not totally comfortable with all this omega stuff," he admitted in a small voice. "I'm barely used to heats, and I've had those for years."

"That's okay." I ran a hand up and down his bare back, enjoying the way he shivered in the embrace. "We can figure all of this out as we go. The important thing is that you'll tell me if something is too much."

"I can do that," he promised, licking over my lower lip and pulling me into another toe-curling kiss.

Running a hand through his hair, I added, "And on your next heat, no running. You let me take care of you, understand?"

He leaned back out of my reach with a smirk, playing thoughtful as he arched his back and let his tantalising nipple piercings twinkle in the light. "You saying I have to retire the knotted dildo?"

"Don't be ridiculous," I scoffed, yanking him back and playfully swatting his arse. "I love to use toys on you. I can picture you now, bound and desperate, dripping with slick, while you try to take a knot at both ends."

Heat pooled low at the thought, and I felt Trystan grow hard against me. As I ran my thumb over his bottom lip, he wrapped his lips around it and sucked. The sensation travelled straight to my rapidly hardening cock.

Pressing down on his tongue, I asked, "Do you like the sound of that, love?"

He nodded, moaning around the digit as he held onto my forearm with both hands. I let him pull my arm down, dragging my thumb over his pouty lip, then his chin, and rested my hand at the base of his throat. His pulse danced beneath my fingertips, and I could feel my own heart matching his, beat for beat. Would I ever get used to being so close to him? I hoped not. I wanted to feel this excitement every second I spent with him.

"I want you to claim me, Emerson," Trystan said, slowly rolling his hips against mine. "Make it so everyone knows I'm yours."

My heart caught in my throat. A bond mark would make him mine for life, no matter what. "Are you sure, love? It's a huge step, and I don't want to push you—"

"You're not," he insisted, digging his fingers into my arm. "Every instinct I have is screaming at me to let you in, and I'm ready to dive off this cliff with you. Be my alpha, please. Bite me."

My already fragile restraint took another gut-punch. Sliding my hand up, I tightened my fingers around his neck enough to hold him securely but not cut off airflow. His pulse quickened, and I crept my spare hand down his back, under his sweatpants and boxers, to gently rub across his hole. He was already leaking slick. I dipped my finger in with ease, dragging a delicious moan out of him that vibrated against my hand. How was I supposed to resist this?

Tilting his head to one side, I breathed along the juncture between his neck and shoulder. Trystan's intoxicating vetiver scent intensified with every movement of my finger against his hole, begging me to sink my teeth into him. A soft whimper squeaked out of him as I grazed my teeth over the spot where I'd mark him.

"I'm going to claim you, Trystan," I promised. "But you're going to wait until this beautiful arse is swallowing every inch of my knot, like a good omega."

"Fuck, yes." His hands released my arm, reaching down to yank my belt open. "Give it to me, alpha, please. You know I can take it."

"I do, love. You take it so well for me. Tell me, which room is yours?" I asked, tightening the arm still fingering him as I stood, holding him like the horny brat he was. "If anyone were to come in and see you like this, I'd be very upset. Understand, love?"

He nodded in my grip, reflexively wrapping his legs around me. "End of the hallway, next to the bathroom."

"Good boy."

Chapter Fifteen

Trystan

E MERSON CARRIED ME TO my bedroom like a starving man heading to a feast, and I was fucking thrilled. He accepted me. I didn't know if I'd be able to get out of thievery for him, but knowing I had the freedom to live my fucked-up life with him was a relief. I was more than a thief to him. And I was more than an omega. He wanted all of me, regardless of the mess it brought.

After all, without that mess, we wouldn't be here.

My back hit the bed, and I looked up to see Emerson yanking off his tie. He smirked down at me, his trousers already half open from my desperation, with an impressive tent poking out. "You have ten seconds to strip and hold your knees beside your head. I'll still knot you all night if you fail, but I won't let you come until dawn. Go."

I couldn't have been more motivated if my life were at stake. Without even getting off the bed, I shucked everything off my hips and kicked it across the room, then assumed the position asked of me.

Emerson chuckled as he carefully folded his clothes, neatly placed them on a chair, and climbed between my spread legs. He tapped his cock against my hole, then ground the thick length of it up and alongside my own, leaning to kiss up my chest.

"So close. Don't fancy being my good little cockwarmer for the night, do you?"

"Mm, actually, that part sounded great." I moaned as he took one of my nipple piercings between his teeth. "It was the threat of all-night edging that made me pick up the pace. Maybe we start with a cheeky one-minute edge and work our way up?"

"Don't worry, love." He planted a kiss on my forehead, and I melted into the pillows. Little moments like that were so unlike anything I was used to, and it never failed to affect me. "I'm going to take such good care of you tonight. Now, where's your lube?"

Within moments of handing him my dwindling supply, Emerson was already two-fingers deep and making me writhe beneath him. I swear, the way he moved his fingers was like he had a fucking built-in map to my prostate.

He circled my Adam's apple with his tongue, kissing along my jaw as he added a third finger. "You need to relax, sweetheart. You're always so tight."

My cock twitched as he fingered me, sparking pleasure all the way down to my toes. "I can take it, please."

Removing his fingers, Emerson lubed his cock and lined up at my hole. He pressed against me, teasing me with his girth as he ran his hands up the backs of my thighs to where I held them up. His hands covered mine, and he leaned down, pushing my legs back further and opening me up to him.

"Ready, love?"

I'd never been more ready in my life. It was scary how quickly my life had changed, but I didn't want to go back now.

"Ready, Alpha."

Emerson entered me in one long, deep stroke, filling me perfectly and making my omega purr. I'd never had this with another partner. No one else praised me or touched me with the reverence he did. Even when he leaned into the dominant side of his alpha, he prioritised my pleasure, and ultimately, my wellbeing. He genuinely cared for me, and I wasn't totally sure what to do with that.

I'd never cared what anyone thought of me before, but the opinion of this man—my alpha—now mattered more to me than I'd ever thought possible. I'd do anything within my power to be worthy of his affection.

His thrusts pounded against my prostate like it had personally offended him, each plunge sending shockwaves of pleasure throughout my body. The scent of leather and patchouli washed over me, and my eyes zeroed in on the juncture between his shoulder and neck.

Bite. Claim.

The urge built inside me like water behind a dam, and I knew I didn't have long until it broke free.

"Please, Alpha," I whined. "Knot me. Claim me."

Emerson pressed his lips to my forehead, my mouth, then my neck. He breathed in deeply, taking in my scent, and a growl rumbled from his chest.

My heart pounded in my throat as the pressure of his knot pushed inside me, stretching me to my absolute limits. Finally, his teeth sank into my neck, and I couldn't have held back my release if I'd tried. Pleasure drowned my senses, overwhelming every nerve ending in my body.

I collapsed into the mattress, my limbs trembling in a tangled heap around my alpha, who licked at the mark on my neck. One prominent urge remained. Summoning my remaining energy, I tangled a hand in the soft strands of Emerson's hair and tilted his neck to the side.

Arms curled beneath me, lifting me to his neck, and I bit down, hard. As my teeth pierced his skin, I instantly felt the change. The bond between us snapped into place, and a strange calm washed over me. All the noises of the outside world faded until it was just me and Emerson, our hearts beating together in perfect synchronicity.

My alpha roared in my arms, his knot throbbing inside me as he emptied himself. My inner omega purred at the sensation of him filling me. Emotions flooded into me, connecting me to my alpha in more than a physical sense. I felt his protectiveness, his loyalty, his love, all pouring into me.

It was the most peaceful I'd ever felt.

I'd woken beside Emerson a few times now, but this morning was different. I felt lighter, somehow. This time, I was his, and he was mine. Fully and completely. I belonged to someone, but not as a possession or a means to an end. With Emerson, I was an equal. He treasured me in a way I'd never experienced before.

Hopefully, I'd get to experience it for a long time to come.

A large, muscled arm tightened around me, pulling me back against my alpha as he kissed across my shoulder to his bite mark. The muscle there ached, but not uncomfortably. More in the pleasurable way I felt after a seriously good fuck. Sore yet sated.

"Morning, love," he murmured against my neck. "How are you feeling?"

"Mm, so good. I always..." I yawned to cover myself before I said something I'd regret. Wiggling back further into his warm embrace, I said, "Yeah, I'm good. You?"

Emerson paused in his gentle kisses before pushing me onto my back and pinning me down with his hips and a curious look. "What was that? You were going to say something else."

"Was not."

A grin spread across his cheeks as he leaned down to lick and nibble along my jaw to my earlobe. "Come on. You can tell me."

"Mm, is this how you get your clients to spill their secrets? I feel like I should be jealous." My hands wandered down Emerson's back, the muscles hard against my palms as I reached the curve of his arse.

Rolling his eyes, Emerson grabbed my wrists and held them firmly beside my head. "Stop changing the subject and tell me. 'You always' what?"

I huffed a breath, avoiding eye-contact. "I always sleep better next to you." Heat spread up my cheeks in a burning glow, and I caught Emerson's eyes practically twinkling in delight. I tried to wriggle out of his grip, but he was so fucking strong. Stupid alpha. "No, no! Stop with the *face*! If you tell anyone I said that, I swear I'll deny it."

Arms curled beneath me, scooping me up like I wasn't a six-foot man with a decent amount of muscle, and rolled me on top of my alpha. Running a hand through my hair, Emerson admitted, "I sleep better with you, too. Your scent relaxes me like nothing else. Holding you is…" He paused, studying my face with a content smile across his lips, "Holding you puts everything in perspective. It means I can sleep, because the only thing that truly matters is safe in my arms."

My words caught in my throat. No one had ever said anything like that to me before, but I felt the truth ringing through his words thanks to our new bond. The force pulling us together was oddly reassuring, like a second set of instincts I could put all my trust into.

Settling on Emerson's chest, I asked, "Do you need to go into the office today?"

"Yes, I need another day to investigate the diary," Emerson explained with a sigh. "Then tonight, we're going to come up with a plan of what to do about your contract with the diary and your employer. Okay?"

My eyes flicked up to his face. "You really think you can get me out of this?"

"I know I can. Your omega trusts me, right? So, if nothing else, trust your own instincts."

I nodded, forcing a smile. "All right. Tonight, it is."

I'd already pushed this job over a week. What harm was one more day?

Emerson reluctantly left my flat far too early for my liking. My omega wanted to spend the day in bed with him, solidifying our new bond. Yet despite my insistence that he looked better naked, Emerson needed to go grab a clean change of clothes before work. At least I could look forward to ripping a different shirt off him later on.

Ooh, I should surprise him tonight. Keep him on his toes.

Wait. Was this how normal people felt? Disappointed to watch their partner leave for the day, yet eager to see them later? Maybe there really was hope for me to have a life with him, away from thievery. Emerson seemed to believe it.

123

Maybe I had a chance.

After choking down some suppressants, showering, and throwing on yesterday's jeans with an old t-shirt, I shuffled to the kitchen in search of Emerson's apology-pancakes. Bee's bedroom door was still open, and I assumed they hadn't come home last night. Or, if they did, they *nope'd* straight back out once they heard the sounds we were making. I probably owed them dinner for that.

As I heated the pancakes, my hand drifted to the bite mark at the base of my neck. My shirt obscured most of it, and it still stung a little when I moved, yet it was oddly comforting to touch. In a few weeks, it would heal into a beautiful silver scar, matching Emerson's.

A knock at the front door snapped me out of my thoughts, and I turned the heat off my food. My gut churned as the hairs on the back of my neck stood on end. Still, I quietly approached the door and glanced through the peephole.

Fucking hell.

"I know you're there, Trystan!" the one voice I'd wanted to avoid taunted through the door. "Time we talked, don't you think?"

Shit, my phone was in my bedroom. I didn't have time to run. All I could do was—

The knocking resumed, louder this time. In a snap decision, I opened the door, forcing the cocky grin my guests were used to seeing.

"Hey, Roman. Leo. You two don't usually make house calls."

"You're right. I don't." Roman smirked wickedly, a flash of overly white teeth. "Good to see you know where this is going, then."

They pushed their way into the flat, and I automatically moved aside, mentally kicking myself for not blocking the door. As Roman made himself comfortable on the sofa, with Leo standing behind him like a menacing shadow, I pulled over Bee's desk chair and took a seat opposite them.

"Ready to start the yelling, Daddy?" I asked, leaning back in the chair partly to appear relaxed, and also to keep my face a little further out of arm's reach.

"Have you ever known me to yell, Trystan?" Roman asked, knowing full well the answer was *fuck yes*. "Don't get me wrong, I'm not impressed right now, but this client ain't exactly my favourite person either. Won't stop calling me for updates, three times a fucking day minimum."

Practically on cue, Roman's phone rang, and he rolled his eyes, pulling the phone out to show me the caller ID—just one letter, H.

"Y'see what I mean?" He scoffed and handed the phone to Leo, who within three long strides was down my hallway, taking the call in a hushed tone. "That fucker won't stop calling me because of your shitty work. I can't have that. He says he needs that diary before he ends up like his missus, but I'm half-tempted to put him out of his misery the old-fashioned way to shut him up." He held his hand to his head like a gun, miming a shot as he cackled at the idea. "Now, Miranda, she was worth the effort. Paid on time, gave me space to make her deliveries. But her man? Clearly not the brains of the operation. Still don't know how we work."

Roman shook his head, tutting under his breath before focusing back on me. "So, with all this push from the client, I wanted to check on you."

"How kind," I choked out, the words making me want to vomit.

"Yeah, see, I've been worried. Your work's usually so solid, so dependable. But this job..." He waved his hands in the air, searching for the words. "It's got the better of you, somehow. You wanna tell me why?"

Keeping my face neutral, I shrugged, meeting his cold eyes dead-on. I'd never flinched before this job, and I wasn't starting now. "Your client underestimated the security of the target. Bad information leads to delays. You know this."

"Bad information, hm. Yeah." He nodded, stretching his arms back behind his tattooed head. "And here I thought it was the alpha you've been fucking all week."

My stomach sank to my arsehole as Roman chuckled, pointing his index finger at me. "Surprised? So was I when the client told me. Turns out, not all his information's bad."

I gnawed on my lip, desperately trying to think of a way out of this that didn't put Emerson in danger. "My sex life doesn't—"

"You one of those omegas?"

I froze, my pulse hammering in my neck, making the claiming bite ache. I hadn't expected him to just come out and ask like that. He'd know if I lied to him, too.

Apparently, my silence was enough of an answer for him.

"I fucking knew it." Roman leaned forward, resting his elbows on his knees as he scrubbed a hand down his face. "After all these years, y'know, I didn't think you'd lie to me about something like this. Guess that's what I get for putting my faith in you. Instead of a professional, I get a goddamned cum-addicted whore."

He rose from the sofa, and my adrenaline spiked. I rushed to my feet, making it two swift steps towards the kitchen for some kind of weapon before a thick arm swooped around my neck from behind.

Fuck! I hadn't even heard Leo come back!

Throwing my elbow behind me, I prayed to hit something that would slow him, but he already had me. Leo's grip around my neck tightened, his forearm constricting my airway as he yanked me back against him. No matter how much I fought, the fucking gorilla of a man barely flinched.

"Y'know, situations like this is why I only hire betas. They're so much easier to control." Roman stepped up close to me, grabbing my jaw painfully tight to force me to look at him snarling in my face. "You owed me *everything!* Did that alpha even have to try to get you in bed with him? Or did you smell him and just offer yourself up? You omegas are fucking pathetic. But I'll still get my money's worth outta you."

He stepped away with a grin, nodding to Leo.

Panic surged through me, and I resumed my struggle, kicking and wriggling for all it was worth. "What are you—"

A sharp sting in my neck cut off my words, and suddenly, my body felt like it was made of lead. My flat spun around me. My knees slammed against the floor, and I landed in a crumpled heap of limbs.

"Careful, Leo!" Roman's voice pierced the fog steadily consuming my mind. "That boy's expensive."

Carpet scratched my cheek as rough hands threw my limp form over something hard, probably a shoulder. Darkness blurred my vision, and I desperately tried to focus on the noises around me, fighting whatever drug was swirling in my system, but it was no use.

"Call the client back. Tell him we've got another to go with his girl, then go collect the diary. I want this job finished today."

CHAPTER SIXTEEN

A

EMERSON

FOR THE FIRST TIME in weeks, I was able to work in the office uninterrupted. I hadn't seen Pearl as I came in this morning, but she was doing an excellent job at herding Harris away from my office all morning. Hopefully, he hadn't asked too much of her yesterday. I'd have to check on her at lunch.

Pushing my colleagues to the back of my mind, I poured my focus into Miranda Fisher's diary. Everything from the text itself to the peculiar wear and tear of certain pages held my interest, but I made a note of a few things I thought could prove useful.

There were many initials we hadn't been able to assign to known associates of hers—R and L were often in short meetings every few weeks, but H seemed to be for social occasions and larger gatherings. Strange that we hadn't found them during the raid where she was arrested.

As I turned the final page, the inside cover caught my eye. The lining curled away from the edge, ever so slightly. Normally, I wouldn't think anything of it in a book this worn, but it was curling away from the spine as if it had been glued down badly in the past. Flipping the book over, I compared it to the inside of the front cover. The edge where the outer cover met the inner lining was sealed perfectly. How odd.

I took a moment to take a few photos on my phone, then grabbed a craft knife from my drawer and carefully peeled up the inner lining of the back cover. It came off with very little resistance, only reaching near the spine all the way down. It definitely wasn't sealed by a professional bookbinder. As I lifted the lining further, it revealed a photograph of a woman, held in the arms of a man, her legs wrapped around his waist as they smiled lovingly at each other.

The woman was instantly recognisable to me from the years' worth of evidence I'd been looking into. Miranda Fisher. But the part that had my hand shaking and my lungs gasping for air was that I also recognised the man holding her. In fact, I saw him just yesterday.

Loving you always, H xx

His handwriting was on the back of the photograph. So familiar and yet... It couldn't be. I must've missed something. There was just no way, right?

My phone clicked over and over as I photographed my findings. This had to be why Trystan was hired to steal the diary. If the police had already found this, he would've been arrested weeks ago. He knew I'd figure this out.

"Emerson!" a muffled voice shouted from outside as a fist pounded on the door. "I need to talk to you!"

"Just a moment!" I called out to the stranger at my door. Where had Pearl gone?

While the banging continued, I quickly placed the photo and fake lining back in the book and locked it away in the small safe under my desk. It would have to do for now.

I practically ripped the door off its hinges as I opened it, knowing I likely looked a mess. My eyes darted around the empty hallway, and I felt sweat beading on my forehead.

An orange blur burst into my office, screaming, "Trystan's gone!"

"Bee?" I spun to Trystan's flatmate, closing the door behind them. "What are you talking about? Slow down."

They looked even worse than I did, clutching a beat-up-looking laptop like a lifeline as they paced in a tight circle on my rug. Reaching out with one hand, I guided them to the sofa.

"What's this about Trystan?" I asked. "He seemed fine when I left this morning. Did he say something?"

Shit, I'd heard of this happening—omegas getting scared after bonding with an alpha if they were left alone too quickly. I hadn't even considered it would happen to Trystan. He seemed so secure in himself earlier. Why would he run?

Bee opened their laptop and clicked through a few folders. "I was showing the audio-bug tech to a friend of mine early this morning, you know, the stuff we used yesterday. Anyway, I realised it was recording live. I thought Trys must've left it in his pocket—he's always doing shit like that—and maybe I'd hear something funny to joke about later..." They inhaled a shaking breath and looked at me with tears in their eyes. "I think he's in real trouble."

"Play it," I said, my jaw clenching painfully. If Bee was reacting this badly, this was something a lot worse than post-bonding jitters.

Bee opened the file, and an unfamiliar voice growled through the laptop's speaker. *"—fucking pathetic. But I'll still get my money's worth outta you."*

"What are you—"

Rage bubbled inside me, burning through my stomach. That was Trystan's voice being cut off, no doubt about it. I wanted to puke.

"Careful, Leo! That boy's expensive."

My heart stopped as rustling sounds and a pained moan filled the audio. What the hell were they doing to him?

"Call the client back. Tell him we've got another to go with his girl, then go collect the diary. I want this job finished today."

Bee closed the lid on the laptop. "There's not much more after that, mostly just some rustling. I found the device still recording at the flat, so they emptied his pockets before leaving with him."

I couldn't breathe. I couldn't blink. My alpha wanted to roar and rip out the throat of the person who would dare to take my omega away from me, but I needed to find them first. More importantly, I needed to know Trystan was safe.

"Do you recognise who took him?"

"Roman. I've only met him a couple times, but he's the one ordering Leo around." Bee swallowed, gripping the sides of the laptop hard enough the plastic creaked. "Why would they take him? I thought Trystan was valuable enough working for them."

"Their client is part of a market that deals in omegas. Probably thought they'd make more money selling him than using him for jobs." Bile rose in my throat at the thought of what they planned for Trystan. The testimonies from Fisher's surviving victims had been harrowing enough without picturing *my* omega in the same situation. "What time did you find that recording?"

Bee glanced at their phone before responding. "About two hours ago. It took me a while to get home and find the flat empty. I came straight here after."

I shot to my feet, heading straight for my desk. "Shit. He could already be here. Check the door!"

Quickly punching in the safe's combination, I grabbed the diary and tucked it under one arm, covering it in my blazer. Not ideal, but it would do for now.

Bee shut the door again before calling out, "The hallway's clear, but we should probably leave your very-well-signposted office."

"Right, stay close to me."

We made our way out of the office, past Pearl's empty desk. Strange. I wondered if she even came into work today but didn't dwell on the thought. We continued moving swiftly towards the elevators until I spotted a hulking man in cargo pants sneering down at a sweating analyst. I ducked into an empty meeting room, pulling Bee with me.

"Was that him?" I asked, already fairly certain of the answer.

Bee nodded, carefully poking their head around the door. "Yeah, the fucker blocking the way to the lifts. Pretty sure he grew a muscle for every spelling test he got wrong as a kid. Still doesn't even know what letter his name starts with."

"I can work with that." I thrust the diary into Bee's hands. "Take this and go up one flight of stairs to boardroom three. It'll be to the right of the lift. Barge into that meeting. They'll yell, but I know you can handle it. Give this to Norah. Don't let anyone else touch it, understand? Only her."

"Got it."

"Tell her I said to look at the photo in the back cover and call detective Rhodes."

Bee looked down at the green book in their hands, their brow furrowed seriously. "But what about Trystan? It's the only leverage we have over whoever has him. We can't give it back to the police."

"You know I'll do anything to get him back, Bee. It's why you came here today. Trust me, this is how we'll do it."

They took a moment to absorb my words, but I had faith. If Trystan trusted them, I would too. Without question.

Shuffling on his feet, Bee asked, "You alphas, uh… You get kinda crazy when your omega is in danger, right?"

I nodded, wondering where this was going. It was difficult enough keeping my alpha urges under control in this situation. The last thing I needed was a reminder.

Bee chuckled, slapping me on the shoulder. "Well, a few years ago, Leo broke Trystan's nose. Have fun with him, 'kay? Meet you upstairs."

My lips spread into a grin as I felt a switch flip in my brain. *Oh, this fucker's gonna pay in blood for touching my omega.*

I approached the desk in long strides, flexing my hands by my sides. Placing one hand on Leo's shoulder, I gently turned him away from the poor analyst and said, "Mike, call security."

As I turned back to Leo, I could practically see a circular buffering logo in his bloodshot eyes. He snarled towards me, and I gave him my most professional smile as I squeezed his shoulder slightly.

"Hello, my name's Emerson Richter. I believe you've been looking for me. Now, I'm told you have someone important of mine. Tell me where he is, and you might get to leave this building with some of your teeth still in your mouth."

Shaking off my hand, he cracked his knuckles. It would've been intimidating if I didn't more than match his size. And this man didn't smell like an alpha. "How 'bout you gimme the diary, and no one 'ere gets hurt?"

Summoning my inner-Trystan, I pretended to think for a moment. "Hm, can't say I know of any book here, at least not one with enough pictures for you to be able to read. I do know of a lumbering idiot already on his last warning, though. Maybe you know him? Huge frame, terrible breath, learned to tie his shoes last week?"

His fist met my lip, and I tasted blood. Perfect.

I chuckled, wiping my chin with my thumb as I leaned into my alpha instincts. "Oh, I'm so glad you threw the first punch. Now, I get to do this."

He dodged my first punch, but he didn't expect the second one to hit him square on the nose. It crunched under my knuckles as the perfect sound of payback, but I didn't ease up. My fists kept swinging until he was on the ground, his breathing reduced to a wet wheezing.

As security finally crowded behind me, I squatted next to Leo, looking him up and down. He'd live, unfortunately.

"You're going to have a hell of a time dealing with assault charges against a lawyer. So, if I were you, I'd start talking." Fisting his shirt, I tugged him off the ground enough to growl in his face, pushing every drop of alpha fury into my words. "Tell me, where is Trystan? Where the fuck is my omega?"

CHAPTER SEVENTEEN

TRYSTAN

THE AIR WAS STICKY and damp on my skin when I woke up. I didn't have the energy to open my eyes, but I could feel my pulse throbbing in my forehead. Weird. I didn't remember drinking. Didn't remember much of anything after Emerson went to work.

Wait. I'd showered—had to clean up after the night we'd had. Then pancakes, but I didn't get to eat them. My stomach cramped. I definitely hadn't eaten in a while. But why didn't I...

The door. Roman.

Fuck.

I forced my eyes open and took in my situation. Whoever brought me here had dumped me on my stomach, and judging by the numbness in my cheek against the concrete floor, I'd been here a while. My lack of movement and the pain in my biceps meant my hands were bound behind me. Why was this becoming a familiar way for me to wake up? But unlike last time, whatever held me pulled at the skin of my wrists and ankles. Ah, my old friend, duct tape.

A soft, familiar voice reached my ears. "Trystan? A-Are you awake?"

Craning my neck, I searched for the source of the voice and spotted a small blond curled in the corner. "Pearl? Fuck, what are you doing here?"

She looked awful. Hair that had previously been in a tight, high ponytail was dishevelled around her pale face, barely held up by the light pink scrunchie atop her head. Dark circles surrounded her eyes, a mix of a lack of sleep and the remains of makeup. Dirt covered her pastel leggings and sweater. How long had she been here?

Pearl's lip quivered. "I don't know. I was helping out after-hours yesterday, then I was gonna go to the gym. He offered me a lift, and I got in the car, but...everything's fuzzy after that. I woke up here alone, and I've been so scared..."

She sniffed, and her body shook, but she looked too dehydrated to cry. Rolling up into a sitting position, I bum-shuffled over to her and leaned next to her, attempting an awkward, armless hug.

"Hey, it's okay. We're gonna be okay, Pearl." I pressed my cheek on the top of her head as she leaned into me, sniffling quietly. As shitty as our situation was, at least she seemed to find some comfort in my presence.

The room we'd been left in was sparse, nothing but a concrete floor and a table and chairs in the middle of the room. Hell, we didn't even have flattened cardboard to sit on. Worst basement prison ever.

A tiny window—too small for me to climb through, but possibly big enough for Pearl—let in sunlight from the top of the wall opposite the stairs. I doubted the door up there would be unlocked, but we'd need to get free of the tape before we could find out.

"We need something sharp to break through the tape. Look around for a stone, a wire, anything with an edge will work."

Pearl's eyes lit up. "Oh! I have a key inside my scrunchie."

My brain took a second to reboot. I'd never heard those words in that order before.

"You what?"

She grinned and pushed her head against the wall, rubbing her ponytail back and forth, steadily loosening it. "There's a pocket in my scrunchie I keep my spare house key in. Some jerk stole my bag at the gym a few years back, so I've always kept a spare for emergencies and for going on runs."

"You're a fucking genius."

Leaning over her, I bit her scrunchie, feeling the key inside the soft material against my teeth, and pulled it off her hair. Spitting it out, I dropped it into her waiting hands behind her back. "Stab the tape and get yourself loose."

She didn't waste any time, immediately yanking the tiny zip open and pulling out the key. "What about you?"

"I'm okay. I'll wait. Focus on yourself right now."

As I rested against the wall, breathing deeply to try to ease the relentless pounding in my head, I watched her saw at the edge of her bonds. Pearl didn't deserve to be here. I was stuck because of years of bad decisions, but she was a good person who worked to help people. How the hell were we in the same shitty situation?

"So, you're an omega, too, hm?" I asked, once again the king of small talk.

Her eyes flicked up to me. "He wouldn't have taken me if I wasn't. I'm guessing you don't have many omega friends."

"Is it that obvious?"

"Painfully." She scoffed. "You say *omega* like it's a curse."

I raised one eyebrow, looking around the musty cellar. "Have you seen where we are right now? It sure as fuck isn't a gift."

"Depends on how you look at it. Right now, I'd say it's the worst thing to be in the world. But other times..." She finally pulled her hands free with a rip and immediately started on her ankles. "Even though I take suppressants to get through the workday without being distracted by a bunch of alphas, I've embraced my inner omega. I love making my nest when I go into heat, and I love leaning into the side of me that wants to feel safe and cared for. There's nothing wrong with it, and I won't pretend that there is."

Pearl's attitude shocked me. I'd never met anyone so openly proud to be an omega, but it was an obvious thing to hide in my world. Being an omega was seen as a weakness, a liability. But for Pearl, it was an accepted part of her, and of course it was. Alphas didn't feel the need to hide their designation from the world, so why should omegas be ashamed of being what they were?

Emerson accepted me. Bee accepted me. Maybe I could accept myself, too.

"Wait, go back a minute," I said, thinking of what she said before. "Do you know who took you? Roman's client?"

A fierce expression took over Pearl's delicate features as she freed her legs. "Yeah, and I feel like an idiot for trusting him for so long. I called him harmless. How fucking stupid of me."

A click at the top of the stairs snatched our attention, and my heart sank. We were out of time.

I quickly whispered, "Give me the key and pretend to be asleep. When he comes to me, sneak upstairs and go for help."

Pearl nodded, shoving the key into my hands and repositioning the tape around her ankles before lying down with her arms behind her back. Aside from her hair, she looked the same as when I'd arrived.

As the door unlocked and footsteps descended the stairs, I gripped the key in a fist and scooched away from Pearl as much as I could. Hopefully, she'd have enough room to creep out.

Sitting upright against a wall, I waited to greet my captor. Shiny leather shoes caught my eye first, followed by trousers an inch too long in the legs. Emerson was going to be pissed.

Harris quickly zeroed in on Pearl and approached her unconscious-looking form.

"Seriously? You go for the sleeping girl first?" I rolled my eyes with a chuckle. "Roman was right. You really are pathetic without your girlfriend."

Harris turned to me, slowly stepping away from Pearl. "Oh, good. The thief is awake. Well, at least we've found a job for you where you're *supposed* to whore yourself out to anyone who asks."

"You sound jealous. Not been getting any with your girlfriend behind bars?"

He grabbed my hair so suddenly, pulling me inches off the ground, I nearly dropped Pearl's key. "Why don't you shut your mouth until it's ready to be filled, omega slut!"

I shook in his tight grip, unable to get to my knees or get my feet under me properly to take the pressure off my scalp. As I twisted in his hold, my neck strained, and Emerson's mark burned against my skin—a comforting reminder of him, but still a raw wound on my throat.

"What the—? That bastard fucking *claimed* you? Oh, of course he did. Emerson gets the promotions, the fancy office. Why wouldn't he get the omega, too?!" Harris released my hair with a push as he paced back and forth, muttering to himself under his breath.

After a minute of his ramblings, he scrubbed his hands down his tired face and squatted over me. He yanked my head to one side and inspected Emerson's mark closely, a disgusted sneer across his face. "Ugh, it's fine. This is fine. You won't be worth as much, but the mark's fresh. After spending a few heats without your precious alpha, the bond will sever on its own."

My omega prickled at the thought of anyone other than Emerson touching me, especially during a heat, but I held it together on the outside.

"Oh, good. That means you only have to keep Emerson away for a year or so. Totally doable for the obvious brains of the operation like yourself."

"A year? Oh, little omega. You'll be going into heat later tonight." Harris's eyes shone as he pulled a small vial of red liquid from his pocket. "See this? I forget the full name, but Miranda's people called it *ardour*. Amazing stuff, really. Just a teensy-tiny injection of this will force your slutty omega body into heat within minutes."

What the fuck? I'd heard rumours about shit like that, but I didn't think it was real, let alone that fast acting. If this was what they'd been doing to the omegas Emerson was representing in court, Harris knew it worked. Even a dumbass couldn't fuck up a little injection like that.

I swallowed at the gravity of the situation, desperately trying to subtly pull at the tape around my wrists with the key, whilst keeping my eyes away from Pearl so Harris wouldn't suspect she was awake. If she didn't get out now, we likely wouldn't get another chance. Once we were in heat, it would be over for us.

"People pay good money for dark web livestreams of omegas being denied, you know." Harris chuckled, sending a chill down my spine that had nothing to do with the concrete floor. "But don't worry. Once you're begging just right, we'll have plenty of cocks ready to replace your precious alpha. How long is your average heat? Three days, maybe four? How many dicks do you think you could take in four days? And with the number of ardour vials that are stashed upstairs, you'll be in heat a lot longer than that."

Sweat beaded at my hairline as I focused on maintaining eye contact with Harris, even through his threats. The longer he focused on me, the better Pearl's chances of escape. Except for one problem. She wasn't creeping up the stairs. Instead, she carefully picked up one of the rickety chairs and approached the maniac planning to drug us.

Don't be a hero, Pearl. Just get out while you can!

Harris grinned at me, nothing but mania in his grey eyes. "Miranda might be gone, but you and Pearl are gonna earn me the money I need to get her out of there. And you're gonna fucking beg to do it, like a good little omega."

Pearl raised the chair above her head and swung it down hard, slamming it on Harris's back and knocking him to the floor.

He yelled as he hit the concrete but stayed conscious and rolled to his back. Reaching behind him, he pulled a gun from his waistband and aimed it straight at Pearl. "You really shouldn't have done that, you stupid little whore."

I struggled harder against the tape, pushing to my feet as I cried out, "Pearl, run!"

Chapter Eighteen

Emerson

"**S**LOW DOWN, OR YOU'LL get us killed!" Norah shrieked from the passenger seat.

It took a disappointingly short amount of time for Leo to tell us where he'd left Trystan. A few clicks from Bee confirmed the property's owner was my colleague—and the longtime lover of Miranda Fisher—Harris Eaves. What a tragically small world we lived in.

Rhodes arrived to arrest Leo as we were on our way out, requesting we remain available for statements while his people searched for Trystan. While I had faith in him, it would take them too much time to formally question Leo and mobilise a squad to search the property. And I wasn't about to wait around while my omega was in danger.

Bee leaned forward from the back seat. "It's a good thing you guys are lawyers, because that was the third speed camera to catch you just now."

My knuckles whitened around the steering wheel. They still had a few flecks of Leo's blood on them that I was reluctant to wash away just yet. The reminder that I'd at least got a small slice of revenge for my omega helped me stay somewhat calm.

"Doesn't matter. We're out of the city now. It won't be long until we get there."

The car fell into an uncomfortable silence as I exited the motorway, swerved around a roundabout, and headed down an unfamiliar country road. According to the satnav, the address was an old farmhouse in the middle of nowhere. Harris had once mentioned growing up on a farm, but he had no living family to speak of, and he'd lived in the city as long as I'd known him. How long had he been going back there for Miranda?

"Emerson, I don't want to doubt you," Norah said thoughtfully. "But are you absolutely sure it's Harris who has him?"

"You saw the photograph," I growled, not taking my eyes off the road.

Norah pinched the bridge of her nose with a sigh. "I just don't understand how we missed it. He was always asking you for updates on Fisher's case. Not to mention how strange he acted around omega colleagues, especially Pearl. I'd convinced myself he was just a curious beta."

I'd been the same, convincing myself he was just a nosy colleague with a crush on my assistant. Even Pearl herself had said he was harmless.

As I thought of Pearl, I realised that with all the commotion today, I still hadn't seen her. And she hadn't messaged to say she was going to be out of office today, either.

Anxiety clawed at my chest, so I tapped the car's screen to call her. Straight to voicemail. She never turned her work phone off. Even when she was sick, she always made sure it had a full battery in case of some kind of emergency. I somehow doubted that today was the one time she found a healthy work-life balance.

"Fuck!" I slammed my hand against the steering wheel. "Pearl was working late with him last night, and she didn't come in today."

Norah bristled in her seat, her voice turning into a low growl I'd never heard from her before. "You think he's taken her as well?"

"I'll bet you anything that when we find Trystan, we'll find her, too."

We parked at the edge of the property and approached the house on foot, wading through the unkempt fields of waist-high grass. The house itself wasn't faring much better. The wooden window frames and front door were rotten and though the brickwork looked intact, ivy climbed an entire side of the building. There weren't any lights on inside, it may not have even had electricity anymore, but I saw several windows were missing glass. At least we had a way inside.

Bee panted as they struggled to keep up with a pair of determined alphas. "This is his house? And you thought this guy wasn't a criminal for how long?"

"His childhood home, I think," Norah explained as we ducked beside a stone wall, checking again for any signs of people inside. "He must've started coming back here after Fisher's network dissolved. A lot of properties in the city were raided, along with several warehouses, but none like this one."

Creeping closer to the house, I said, "I can only see one car, but let's not count on him acting alone."

We silently approached the wall covered in ivy, peeking around the corner at the muddied Audi parked near the door. I recognised it as Harris's car, and my heart sank a little further. It seemed useless to hope I'd be wrong about him by this point, but still, part of me persisted.

Staying low to the wall, I peeked inside the nearest window. The glass was completely missing, allowing me a perfect view of an old living room. Every surface was smothered in a layer of dust, except a spot on the sofa and footprints around the furniture. I couldn't hear anyone moving around nearby, though. Were they upstairs?

Where *was he?*

My heart was pounding too wildly to know if I was feeling Trystan's nearby anxieties through the bond, or simply my own. Gritting my teeth, I inhaled deeply, desperately searching for even the slightest trace of Trystan's scent. There, beneath layers of dirt, country air, and rotting wood, was the heady mixture my alpha recognised as mine. A cocktail of mint, metals, and vetiver that was entirely Trystan.

"He's here." I felt like I could finally breathe again, knowing I'd be with him soon and there was at least a chance he was okay. "Or at least he was recently. I'm going inside."

"Wait." Norah pulled out her phone, tapped on it, then thrust it into Bee's hand. "Here, take this and go back to the car. It's already dialling detective Rhodes. Tell him to get his arse over here immediately with at least one ambulance." Her eyes flicked to me before she pushed Bee back towards the car and crouched beside me. "Remember, Emerson, we need Harris alive to go through the courts. I know every instinct is telling you to kill him, but do everything you can to hold it back."

"I won't kill him," I promised her. "But if he's done *anything* to harm either of them, I'm going to make sure he suffers as long as possible."

Her grin turned feral, matching my own. "Oh, he'll suffer. I promise you that."

Not wanting to waste any more time now that Bee had gone for help, we hopped in through the empty window. Broken glass littered the floor, impossible to avoid under our footsteps as we crept through the room to an empty hallway.

Norah tapped my shoulder and silently pointed to an open doorway where a clean blazer lay on the back of a chair. As we snuck into the room, empty of recent life except for the jacket, I could hear a muffled voice somewhere nearby.

Trystan's scent was stronger here, the metallic undertones of his scent taking centre stage, likely from the stress of the situation. Letting my alpha instincts take charge and follow his scent, I approached a large wooden door leading further into the house. As I carefully turned the handle, a dark staircase greeted me, along with the snarling voice of my former friend.

"Miranda might be gone," he said, "but you and Pearl are gonna earn me the money I need to get her out of there. And you're gonna fucking beg to do it, like a good little omega."

White-hot rage burned in my chest as I descended the stairs with Norah right on my tail, the two of us abandoning all attempts at stealth in favour of reaching the omegas *now*. We hit the ground in time to see Pearl slam a chair into Harris's back, and my eyes zeroed in on Trystan against the wall.

He's alive!

Despite Trystan's bound limbs, he pushed to his feet, yelling as Harris pulled a gun from his waistband, aiming directly for Pearl. "Pearl, run!"

He launched his body at Harris, knocking him back to the ground in a painful tackle. The gun fired wildly as Norah lunged for Pearl, and I rushed to Trystan, praying that he wasn't hit. As I reached out to grab my omega, a hair's breadth from having him safe in my arms again, he was pulled away from me.

"Don't come any closer!" Harris yelled, one hand around Trystan's throat while the other pressed the gun against his temple. "Get back, or I'll shoot! Now!"

Stepping away from Trystan meant smothering every protective instinct I had as an alpha. I wanted to rip Harris's throat out with my teeth, and I knew I could, given half a chance, but I just couldn't risk him.

"What's your plan here, Harris?" I asked, backing up to the opposite wall next to Norah, who held a shaking Pearl behind her. "There's no way out. Police are already on their way. If you let him go, you'll at least get out of this alive."

Harris scoffed, getting to his feet and pulling Trystan up with him by his neck. "You think I'm an idiot? I've seen the mark on his neck. I know what you alphas will do for one of these whores!"

I know you're an idiot; else you'd know better than to call him that.

Trystan's bright green eyes met mine, and he wriggled in Harris's grasp. If his omega was screaming inside him half as much as my alpha, it must've been maddening. I was one wrong move from going fully feral to get him out of here, my own life be damned.

Was it really only this morning we were together? Newly bonded and excited at the thought of planning a life together? I swore I'd protect him, and I fully intended to keep that promise.

"Then you know that every second you keep him from me endangers you," I growled, baring my teeth. "One last chance, Harris. Let him go."

Harris's eyes darted around the cellar. Norah stood closest to the stairs, ready to get Pearl out at the next opportunity. But Harris would have to go through all of us to get out.

"No, see, you're gonna go keep the police away," he said, his shaking voice betraying the confidence in his orders. "I'm holding the fucking cards here!"

"Bitch, you're not even holding *me*," Trystan sneered as he twisted violently in Harris's grip.

A rip reached my ears, and Trystan's hands separated from behind his back. As one arm stretched up sharply to knock the gun away, he spun to face his captor and thrust his other hand into Harris's face. Norah seized the opening, dragging Pearl upstairs out of harm's way, and I sprinted to my omega.

Grabbing Harris by the collar, I ripped him from the wall and slammed him against the ground with an animalistic roar. His skull cracked against the concrete, and blood poured from his eye, a small key sticking out of it grotesquely. He stopped moving.

"Is... Is he dead?" Trystan panted behind me.

I stared at the man on the ground. We'd never been close—work friends, at best—but I couldn't find any scrap of compassion for him inside me. I wanted to watch him die for what he'd done.

"He's still breathing. Won't be getting up for a while, though."

Trystan slumped against the wall, falling to the floor as he frantically tugged at the tape around his ankles. I quickly pulled it off him, and he launched himself into my arms. Vetiver consumed my senses as I held him close, tangling a hand in his hair and breathing him in like the first time all over again.

"You really came for me," he said, shaking against me.

His relief, his fear, his love slammed against my heart through the bond, and all I could do was hold him through it.

"I've got you, love," I promised, kissing his temple. "I swear, I've got you. You're safe."

CHAPTER NINETEEN

TRYSTAN

"A LL RIGHT. THAT SHOULD do it, Mr Wells."
Detective Rhodes smiled, putting away his phone and closing his notepad.

It had been a long night at the hospital, and an even longer morning as Rhodes took my statement on what happened. He'd offered to let me sleep some more first, but I wanted it over with. The sooner I could move on from this shit, the better.

"That's it? I'm not like"—My eyes flicked to Emerson, then back to Rhodes—"in trouble for anything?"

The corner of Rhodes's mouth quirked, and he tapped his chin with the notepad, choosing his words carefully. "While the recording provided by your friend certainly shows intent to steal evidence, you technically didn't commit any actual crime we can see. Also, Emerson made a compelling argument that with everything you did to help bring in Fisher's associate, as well as getting us enough evidence to arrest one of the city's major crime lords, we can look the other way. Provided, of course, you remain on the correct side of the law in the future."

Looks like I'm retiring early.

Emerson brought my hand to his lips, placing a soft kiss on my knuckles before saying, "Told you I'd sort everything out, didn't I?"

"Yeah, yeah. You were right, I know," I grumbled half-heartedly, squeezing his hand.

Since saving me in the cellar yesterday, Emerson had only left my side once, on the doctor's orders, and even that had taken some convincing. Throughout the night, part of him had always been touching me, whether it was him holding my hand, stroking my hair, or feeling the rise and fall of my chest as I slept. I think he'd needed the reassurance that things were okay as much as I did.

"We shouldn't need anything else from you, but I'll call tomorrow just to check in." Rhodes patted me on the shoulder gently before heading for the door.

"Oh, wait!" I called after him. "Have you heard anything from Pearl? How's she doing?"

"She's shaken and very dehydrated but doing well," he said with a kind smile. "Francis and Norah have hardly left her side. I'll check on her again before I leave and tell her you're thinking of her."

"Appreciate it. Let her know I'll replace her house key as a thank you."

Pretty sure she wasn't interested in getting the key that the doctors had to remove from Harris's eyeball.

The door clicked shut behind the detective, and I leaned back against the small mountain of pillows Emerson had found for me. It was comfortable, but not quite what I needed. Shuffling forwards on the bed, I tugged gently on Emerson's hand.

"Can I help you?" he asked, trying and failing to hide a smile.

"Don't make me say it."

"Only because you were held at gunpoint less than twenty-four hours ago." He climbed onto the bed behind me, legs on either side of my body, and wrapped his big arms around me.

Patchouli washed over me as he held me against his chest, his heartbeat thumping against my back soothingly. It amazed me to think that being in the arms of an alpha used to be my nightmare.

Right now, I couldn't think of anything more perfect.

Still, a thought nagged in my head. "You really think they'll be able to keep Roman behind bars?"

"I think he'll do his damndest to get out, but I know a team of prosecutors who'll make sure he stays put." Emerson cupped my jaw, turning my head to face him over my shoulder. "He's never getting near you again. Same for Harris, if he ever wakes up."

His lips brushed mine, sealing a promise I fully trusted him to keep.

"Thank you. But how are you doing with the Harris stuff?" He raised an eyebrow at me. "Sorry, I just mean you worked with him for a while, right?"

Emerson nodded solemnly. "Years. We started at the firm as interns together, fresh out of university. He never mentioned being in any relationship, let alone with someone like Fisher..."

"It's possible he was hiding it as long as he knew you."

"Exactly." He sighed against me. "I don't know if or when he changed, or whether he was always like that and I just didn't care enough to see it."

I curled into him, gently rubbing my cheek against the skin exposed by his open collar. Scenting him this way made my omega purr, and I hoped it soothed his alpha, too. It was a strange way to comfort someone, but it felt right instinctually.

"You couldn't have changed his mind, Emerson. He was dedicated to her, no matter what."

Eventually, the rhythmic sounds of Emerson's breathing, along with the stress of the past day, sent me back to sleep. Turns out, I really did sleep better with him around, even in a hospital. It was like my body had finally come out of fight or flight after so many years, and I could simply exist.

By the time I came round again, someone else was in the room talking to Emerson. He wasn't being unnecessarily hostile, so not a doctor here for more "just in case" tests. That left...

"Hey, Trys. Good to see you awake." Bee grinned at me. "But damn, you look like shit."

"Aww, that means we finally match."

"Oh, so witty." They rolled their eyes, then leaned down to grab a tote bag and held it up like Simba at Pride Rock. "Guess that means you're not interested in a bag of clean clothes to go home in?"

"I take it all back, oh gracious bringer of pants."

Bee's arrival apparently made Emerson comfortable enough to go check in on Pearl and fetch us some decent coffees from across the street. It warmed my heart to see him so accepting of my best friend.

While we had a few minutes alone, I had something I needed to say to them. "I forgot to say it yesterday, but thanks for finding me, Bumble. I don't know where I'd be without you."

Bee scratched the back of their neck, a crooked smile across their face. "Eh, alpha-man gets most of the credit. But he wouldn't have known you were gone so quickly without me, so I'll take that instead. I'm your unintentional number one stalker."

A laugh burst out of me. Emerson would definitely have something to say about not being ranked first. "Ooh, there're ranks amongst my stalkers now. How exciting. I should make you all t-shirts now that I'm out of a job."

"Or you could shut up and get some rest, idiot," Bee said, oddly seriously. "I need you out of here and ready to work so we can start that P.I. thing for real."

I did a double take. "Wait, you really wanna do that?"

They shrugged their shoulders non-committedly, but their smile betrayed their excitement. "I kinda like the sound of legitimate income. Plus, with some of our new contacts, getting clients should be a breeze."

They had a point. I'd initially dismissed the idea a few days ago as a manipulation from Emerson to get me out of thievery. Now that I understood his motivations, and my favourite partner seemed up for it, could it really be worth a shot?

Emerson came back in before I could give an answer. Bee just waved it off with, "Have a think about it."

A doctor came by to discharge me not long after. It was a relief to change into some clean clothes and be heading somewhere familiar. Pearl had to stay another night, but the nightmare was over.

Emerson opened the passenger door for me, ever the gentleman. "Ready to go home?"

"Definitely. But we're going to my home, right?"

"I just thought since the last time you were there...and, you know, because my place is bigger—"

"I really want to be back in my own bed for a bit," I admitted. "Pretty sure if we went to yours, I'd never leave, and I can't say I'm ready to move in just yet. But I'd really appreciate it if you stayed with me tonight."

It would be tough going back to a flat where I was drugged and kidnapped, but it was also the place where my alpha had claimed me. It had as many good memories as it did terrible ones, and I knew which I wanted to focus on for a change.

Emerson's hands circled my waist, his patchouli scent flaring as he caught my lips in a toe-curling kiss in the car park. I fisted the lapels of his jacket as I returned the kiss, half-tempted to ask if we could use the back seat before we left.

Instead, I let him pull away enough to speak against my lips. "Anything you want, love."

"Mm, you'll regret saying that."

"No, I won't," he insisted. "Listen, you might drive me crazy with your reckless attitude sometimes, and I may make you want to run because I won't leave you alone. But we're mated, and I love you. Therefore, I will never, ever regret anything with you."

My chest swelled with emotions. I could feel his love through the bond but hearing it aloud was so different. He truly accepted me—the omega, the thief, the broken man trying to make it through the day.

"Take me home, Alpha."

Epilogue

A

Emerson

"Everything's going to be fine, love," I said, awkwardly balancing my phone between my ear and my shoulder as I piled my items into the huge reusable bag the cashier had guilted me into buying. Fuck me for leaving my earphones at the office. This was why I worked from home! "I just stopped for a few supplies, but I'm on my way now. I'll be ten minutes max."

The breathless whine that danced along the line between horny and pathetic reached my ears. It had been almost four months since claiming Trystan, and since transitioning onto a real prescription of pheromone suppressants, he was finally having his first heat as a mated omega.

And I was nowhere near him the day it hit.

Logically, I knew it couldn't be helped. Heats were unpredictable, and he'd even said I should go in today because it had been a while. My inner alpha, however, disagreed.

163

There was one person to blame—me—and it was time to do everything in my power to get to Trystan.

I was seriously at risk of losing my licence if I kept driving like this.

It took seven minutes to get to Trystan's flat, and I soared up the stairs to reach my omega. I burst into the flat, a flurry of tote bags and panic as I rushed past Bee to Trystan's bedroom, ready to find it...empty?

"Where the hell is he?" I asked the perfectly made bed, as if he would pop out from underneath like a horny surprise party.

Bee stood in the doorway, headphones around their neck as they leaned against the frame. "That's what I was trying to tell you when you stormed past. He's not here."

"That doesn't tell me where he *is!*" I growled.

Bee held up their hands in surrender, eyes wide as they shrank back against the wall. They were saved only by my phone ringing. My shoulders immediately relaxed when I saw my omega's photo on the screen, and I hit 'answer'.

Trystan screamed through the device. "Where are you?"

Funny, that was my question.

"I'm at your flat. Where are you?"

"Why the fuck are you there?" he asked, like I'd made the stupidest move of my life. "I'm in your bedroom! I've been doing that nesting bullshit you said would make me feel better, but all I feel is..." His voice trailed off for a moment, until his fire burst forth again. "Just tell me when you're getting here."

The drive across the city had never felt longer, but I made it in record time. I rushed through the foyer and barely managed to stand in one place through the elevator ride to my floor. But when I reached my bedroom, the place we'd first kissed after I'd scented him as my match, I stopped for a moment.

Standing in the doorway, I admired my omega curled amongst the mound of cushions and pillows. Some of them I'd bought immediately after meeting my omega, others I didn't even know I owned. All of them, everything I owned, were for him.

Finally, I couldn't resist him anymore. I kicked my shoes off and straddled his waist in his nest, kissing up his neck and licking over the claiming mark I'd left on him four months ago. "You made your nest here."

Trystan gasped under my touch, fisting my hair and bucking his hips. He was already hard beneath his sweatpants. "Yeah, I know."

"You made it *here*."

"Yes, we've established that." He stared at me with both eyebrows raised. "Why are you repeating yourself when you could be stripping?"

Ignoring his question, I cupped his face and peppered it with kisses, never staying in one spot long enough for him to get his bearings. "Love, it means you feel safe with me."

Trystan pulled away, his brow furrowed and eyes dark. Shit, did I overstep?

"Of course I feel safe with you, Emerson. I wouldn't let you within ten feet of me if I didn't!"

He pushed on my shoulder, rolling us over to put him on top. Our lips met in a hungry clash of teeth and tongue as our scents curled around each other. Vetiver and patchouli. An earthy mix of smoke and spice.

Trystan ground his hips down on my own, our clothed erections rubbing deliciously as he spoke. "You are my alpha. Therefore, when I'm in heat, I want to surround myself with your scent, your belongings, your... *You*. I love you."

I dragged him down for another kiss, tasting him for what felt like the first time all over again. "I love you too, Trystan. So fucking much."

"Can I please ride your knot, Alpha?"

Hm, he did ask nicely. But...

Rolling us back over, I flipped Trystan onto his stomach, dragged down his sweatpants, and cracked my hand down on his arse with a reverberating smack. "I have so many plans before we get to that, love."

Acknowledgements

I want to kick off my thank you's with a huge shout-out to Crystal North, because without her, this book wouldn't exist. Thank you for pushing me into trying a fun new genre, for answering my many, many questions, and for being so incredibly supportive throughout this process.

Incredible thanks to the wonderful ladies of Indie Love Wales. These writing retreats and dinners have done wonders for my mental health, my motivation, and really made me feel like part of something special. Thank you for lovingly peer pressuring me into success. I love you all!

To my online author besties, Emmy Dee and TL Hamilton, I wouldn't be able to get through the day without you guys. I can't wait to give you both the biggest, squishiest hugs of all time, but I'll settle for memes at all hours of the day until then.

Lastly, thank you to everyone who picked up *Therefore*. You all allow me the freedom of hopping between genres depending on how my muse is feeling, and writing what I want. Thank you for giving Trystan and Emerson your time and I truly hope you enjoyed their story.

This won't be the last omegaverse you see from me, but who knows what else is on the way?

ALSO BY KATHERINE ISAAC

MOON DUST LIBRARY
Paranormal Polyamorous Standalone
Moonlit Agate
Paranormal M/M Prequel (Can be read as standalone)
Twisted Fate

THE CURSED COVEN OF SPELLS HOLLOW
Paranormal Polyamorous Romance
Warrior Witch

CONTEMPORARY STANDALONES
Contemporary Polyamorous Romance
The Night Shift Before Christmas

OMEGAVERSE STANDALONES
M/M Omegaverse Romance
Therefore

M/F Hockey Omegaverse Romance

Game On

www.katherineisaac.com

ABOUT THE AUTHOR

Katherine Isaac lives and works in Wales with her beloved cat-son. Growing up surrounded by mythology and history has fueled her love for epic stories of magic, mystery, and romance.

She is happiest with her nose in a book, pinned down by a cat, or surrounded by nature; whether that's lying on the grass or diving in the ocean.

Katherine describes herself as an eternally sleep-deprived pixie, with the mouth of a sailor and too many characters living in her brain.

Join Katherine's Facebook Readers Group to be part of the discussions and sign up for Katherine's newsletter to stay up to date on all the latest news!

Printed in Dunstable, United Kingdom